BEST READ
PRODUCTIONS
PRESENTS...............

A
COLD
PASSION

BY C.&T. THOMAS

CHAPTER ONE

"Don't cry child we all got to go one day. I been on this earth seventy-one blessed years honey and I don't have any complaints." Passion squeezed her grandmother's hand as a tear fell from her eye.
"I know it's hard for you to watch me emerge so close to death but only God knows the time and the hour. Passion you know what?"

"Yes Granny." Passion replied with tears in her eyes.
"I'm eager to meet the Lord. You just do your best down here as a lawyer and be all you can be."
"I will granny I promise."

"I know you will honey," said Granny as she exhaled. Her eyes were getting heavy as sleep was closing in.

"Honey listen, if you allow the ways of the world to get in your way, you will never find happiness. I cannot tell you this enough baby. Always remember to pray no matter what your situation is. Good, bad, happy, or sad, always remember to get down on your knees and pray. Just ask God for guidance and continue to treat folk how you would like to be treated. Since you gone be this 'BIG SHOT' lawyer and all, (granny smiled), always remain humble and understand that this is a blessing. To be a young educated woman in this day in age, is truly a blessing. Another thing Passion. Do you know that the same folks you see going up is the same ones you gone see coming down?"

Graphic Designer Contact Info _jiffygraphics@gmail.com_
Photographer Contact Info phodges27@gmail.com

Library of Congress Cataloging in publication will be available upon request.

This Novel is dedicated to our Family in Heaven. R.I.H. Kenneth Thomas, Howard Hardnett, Paco, Jarvis, Mama Katie, Aunt Cherie, Aunt Rhonda, Uncle Stevie, Uncle Ricky, Grandpa Grady, Gladys aka Mamma, Cousin Stephen, Grandma Ella Mae, Grandpa John, and many more. Gone, but will never be forgotten.

"Best Read Productions would like to thank you

for your support and we hope that this may

influence someone, young or old to embrace the

gift that God has given you. It's never too late to

make it happen"!!!!!!

Passion wiped her tears while sitting at attention.

"Listen to me child and please hold my words in your heart. You never know who may have to give you a glass of water and those small four letters in the word love are the keys to happiness."

Passion stayed with her grandmother until hospital visiting hours were over. Afraid that her grandmother was going to die any day now, she dozed off until it was time to go home.

Last year Mrs. Mamie Veland, was diagnosed with lung cancer and was told she only had six months to live. Although her doctor's prediction was a few months overdue, her illness was now at its worst. Her hair had fallen completely out, and her weight decreased tremendously. Within one year she went from one hundred and fifty-two pounds to one hundred and three. She was tired of fighting the disease and prolonging her death which was now catching up to her at a fast pace. Ever since she was diagnosed, Passion struggled to accept the fact that her grandmother was dying. Grandma Mamie was everything to her since birth.

Passions' biological mother Patricia, was a prostitute on drugs from the age of thirteen, until her mind slipped one day. Passion was ten years old when her mother was placed in the Asylum never to return home. Due to their estranged relationship, she never allowed herself to deal with her feelings toward her mother's situation.

She loved her mother but hated her as well for not showing that she cared enough before her mental breakdown. Passion never knew who her father was, which was why Patricia decided to give her up for adoption in the first place. Yet what appeared to be the beginning of a disastrous life for Passion, had turned out just fine due to the parental support from her grandmother.

Passion was spoiled growing up. Almost anything she wanted she could have as long as her grades stayed up in school, and she vowed to never stray from her studies for that reason alone. When she reached high school, she developed a desire to become a lawyer. As her desire grew, her determination did as well. Suddenly she was no longer a young girl with an imagination, but a mature teenager with a dream.

Once Mrs. Veland noticed how serious she was about becoming a lawyer, she began to encourage and motivate her. While most teenagers around her age were party goers, drug dealers, promiscuous, and focused on living life in the fast lane, Passion was the total opposite. She confined herself to different libraries, reading law books as if they were novels. As a teenager she had a few friends, but her will to succeed overshadowed those aspects of her life. The only person she considered to be a true friend was a childhood friend named Tiara Wright.

For four years now, her occupation was working as a secretary for a law firm downtown. A law firm with a reputation for keeping the clients free for the right price, and a dirty track record. The defense lawyers she worked for at Peckard Law & Associates were known for using illegal strategies and methods to free their clients, who were mainly murderers, drug dealers, and rapist. Throughout Omaha, Nebraska this law firm was everyone's first option, unless the accused didn't have the financial means to pay for one of his lawyers.

William Peckard, a middle aged white guy with a devious desire to see all his clients go free, and also demanded that same attitude from every lawyer employed at his firm. Most criminals were aware that when dealing with his law firm, they'd have a 70% chance of getting their cases dismissed or proven not guilty. Mr. Peckard was impressed by Passions knowledge of the law. Ever since the day he hired her, he knew she would soon evolve above her position as a secretary to an outstanding attorney. Discreetly, Mr. Peckard planned on tucking her under his wing for keeps.

Passion left the hospital and went home. As soon as she let herself in the door, a strong aroma engulfed her. The smell of Tiara's lasagna made her recognize her hunger pangs. By the radio being up so loud, Tiara didn't hear her entrance as she swayed to the R&B tunes of Calvin Richardson in front of the stove. Passion stood behind her, admiring her flawless figure as she continued to groove and sing the lyrics of the song. Passion needed a good laugh and knew she was about to get one as soon as Tiara turned around. Attempting to scare Tiara, she tossed a pen across the room that hit her on the back of the legs. Tiara quickly turned around dropping the wooden spoon on the floor.

"Now why would you want to just scare me like that?" Passion couldn't stop laughing. "You scared the hell out of me. Now if my heart would've stopped." Tiara uttered while shaking her head. "Taste this and tell me if this is perfection."

Tiara grabbed the spoon and chunked out a piece of her famous lasagna and put the spoon to Passions mouth.

"Wow! This shit taste like you grew up in Italy," said Passion while smacking her lips.

"If this was shit Passy it wouldn't be good now would it? Here's your plate crazy girl!" She'd nicknamed Passion Passy for short.
Passion's smile turned into somewhat of a sad look as she sat down at the kitchen table.

"How is she?" asked Tiara in a low tone. Passion put her head down.

"Physically not good but mentally, she is fine. She's not afraid to die but that's what's giving me the strength to accept this."

Tiara started to massage her neck and shoulders.

"I'm glad you're being strong about this, I know how much she means to you."

A tear rolled down Passion's face.

"It's going to be a different life without having her here. Ever since birth her love for me has been unconditional and that's why I cherish her. How can I let go of something so special?"

"You'll never let her go. Her spirit will live on forever and trust me, she'll be watching your every move from heaven," said Tiara.

Passion looked at Tiara with tears in her eyes and yelled.

"SO, I'M JUST SUPPOSED TO ACCEPT IT RIGHT?"

"You have no choice Passy..........I'm sorry you don't have a choice," Tiara softly whispered.

"Sometimes I don't know what I would do without you. I don't even consider myself a lesbian, what we share is what we share."

Tiara didn't respond as she continued to massage her back. Passion kept her eyes closed and enjoyed the sensation.

"I'm always going to be here for you in every way," said Tiara.

"What if Shawn ever found out that we're more than friends?"

Tiara ignored her question.

"So now you want to be quiet..............That's ok I get it. This is a prime example of having your cake and eating it too," said Passion as she shook her head.

Passion knew how much she loved him, but Tiara didn't love one more than the other.

"Tiara, exactly how long do you expect him to go without at least becoming somewhat suspicious. I mean we've been living together for three years now, and you've refuse to move in with him no matter how much he beg. We do everything together, and I know he can sense a vibe between us when we're all together."

"Listen Passy don't worry about Shawn he's under control. Besides, he probably does suspect something, but as long as it's not another guy that I'm giving his love away to, trust me, he'll be just fine."

"What about your heart, I have that too right?" asked Passion.

"Of course you do silly!" Smiled Tiara.

"Well what if he thought he was sharing your heart with me?"

"Then he would have to make a decision. Enough about him I'm ready to eat and take a shower besides, you look real tasty to me right about now!"

They both giggled and rushed into the bathroom.

Tiara met Shawn at a bowling alley while Passion was away at college. Her light skinned creamy caramel complexion was irresistible to him. She had a voluptuous figure and a pearl white smile you could see from across the room. Her hair had a natural flow that blew with the wind and was cut in layers that she kept neatly flat ironed. To him she looked just like Lisa Raye, and he was dying to get to know her. Shawn approached her with smooth words and a sense of humor. Tiara was immediately attracted to his swag. All she could think about was his clean nails, tight fade, and a smile that would make any women melt. Chemistry quickly sparked, and the beginning of their relationship was set.

When she met him, Shawn didn't have much money as a drug dealer, but after a year into their relationship he connected with a Drug Lord name Shakeem, a notorious boss in the city. Not only did his cash flow sprout, so did his status, nevertheless his heart stayed with Tiara. He spoiled her with fancy cars, expensive jewelry, designer bags, and enough clothing so that she could wear a new outfit for 3 months straight. Every year he upgraded her fashion and accessories with top of the line designers and he never questioned her for wanting to keep her home in the suburbs. Shawn looked at it as a little room to play, but it surprised him a tad bit when she moved her best friend Passion in. Shawn didn't give her a hard time about it. He respected the fact that Passion had just returned home from college. The girls didn't plan on starting a sexual relationship but one night, just like that, Tiara and Passion went from best friends to lovers.

CHAPTER TWO

"Peckard Law & Associates how may I help you? Yes, I'm going to place you on a brief hold while I connect you." After connecting the client to the requested lawyer, Passion sat back in her chair and yawned.

In front of her was a desk full of caseloads that had to be put in order and placed in file cabinets. She was in no rush to complete the task as she daydreamed about her future, visualizing what it would be like to run her own law firm. Passion wasn't slow by any means. She was sure of her capabilities and confident that she would soon make her dreams a reality.

As an intern, Peckard came to her often for strategic advice. At times he would have her write out his closing arguments in advance. The other lawyers weren't fond of her because they knew she would one day be a partner and could possibly cut into their salaries. Truthfully Peckard knew there wasn't an attorney at his firm that could measure up to Passions acumen of law. He was also strongly impressed by the way she organized his closing arguments for him to recite. Her words, phrases, and artistic sensibility painted a picture of pure innocence. Peckard knew that she would be the one that all metro area prosecutors would fear.

In another month she was scheduled to graduate. Passion wasn't worried at all about passing the bar and was extremely excited to fulfill her dream. Having the ability to showcase her true talent as a criminal lawyer was something she had been dreaming about since she was knee high. Becoming a successful black woman let alone an attorney was unheard of in the neighborhood she was raised in.

Out of nowhere sadness overshadowed her mood as thoughts of her grandmother invaded her mind. A lonely feeling washed over her and suddenly she couldn't wait to go see her after her shift ended. A knock at the door grabbed her attention.

"How may I help you?"

"I'm a Client of Ericka Peezie, and I have a meeting with her at two thirty."

"Let me guess, your Chaz Washington, right?"

He nodded.

"She's in a meeting right now, but considering you're a half an hour early, I'm sure you have patience." May I offer you a cup of coffee, tea, or bottled water?"

"No thank you." Chaz replied.

He took a seat by the vestibule. Passion sat back down at her desk and called into Ericka's office letting her know her two thirty client had arrived.

"Ericka's aware of your presence Mr. Washington and will be right with you shortly."

"Thank you!"

Chaz was out on bond for vehicular homicide and his first pretrial was in two weeks. He paid Ericka fifteen thousand to represent him, to see if she could help him beat the case. Twenty-three years old, first offense, and an actual mistake seemed reasonable enough.

Considering Chaz was black, and the victim was a fifty-six-year old Caucasian woman, his chances of having a fair trial were reduced tremendously. He had a license but no insurance. He wasn't drunk when the accident occurred, however he did blow borderline numbers.

Although the lady was at fault, Richard Green who was one of the most feared prosecutors in this jurisdiction, was going to underline and enhance all his flaws. He was seeking a conviction since Chaz wanted to take it trial.

A few minutes later Mr. Peckard came out of his office and walked up to her desk.

"Hey Passion, all of my caseloads for tomorrow must be rescheduled to the fifth of December."

"Ok! I'm on top of that right now sir."

"Oh Passion?"

"Yes!"

Mr. Peckard took three steps back towards Passion with a smile on his face.

"Order a dozen roses and send them to the name and address on this paper."

He handed her a folded slip of paper and went back into his office. By the time three o'clock rolled around, Passion was eager to get off work to go visit her grandmother. Passion and Mr. Peckard left the office together.

"After you graduate next month, do you have a specific law firm in mind?" Passion's eyes were wide open as she hid her wide smile on the inside.

"I would love to hire you on with our team. We could use an extra mind around and I know you would do a brilliant job."

"Well I really."................

"Hold on Passion, before you answer that question give it some thought. This is a very big step and I want you to be certain you've made the right decision." Peckard interrupted.

Passion smiled.

"Well honestly sir, it would be an honor to partnership with this firm."

Mr. Peckard grinned.

"Yes my dear you have a bright future ahead of you, not to mention you're going to be tough to wrestle with in that courtroom. You'll save many lives that most of the time doesn't deserved to be saved. Your goal is to become the client's first choice, and in my book.........You're the chosen one. Welcome to the team." A brief hug was exchanged.

"I'll see you tomorrow Mr. Peckard and thanks for everything. I won't let you down I promise!"

"Your welcome. Drive careful!"

As she drove to the hospital, she visualized herself as an attorney at his firm. The four body personnel were superb at their jobs, but she knew that her ability to think, maneuver, and manipulate the law exceeded her colleagues. A position at his firm would only be a stepping stone for her. She always wanted her own firm and reminded herself that working for others would only be short lived.

****

It was three seventeen when she pulled into the hospital parking lot. As she walked up to the emergency room door trembling with fear, suddenly over the intercom she heard, "Code Blue to room three ten, code blue to room three ten!" At first it didn't register that they were calling her grandmother's room. Passion jumped out of line and ran hysterically down the hall. Before security could stop her, the elevator doors opened, and Passion rushed in frantically jabbing the button to close the door.

As she waited for her floor, she closed her eyes and prayed. "God please don't let this be it." No matter how much she tried to prepare herself for her grandmother's death, it still was a hard pill to swallow. When she stepped off the elevator she observed doctors and nurses coming and going out of room three ten.

A security officer had to refrain her from going inside. As the flat line sounded, she could only watch hopelessly as they tried to revive her. At three twenty-eight her best friend and her everything, Mrs. Mamie Veland was pronounced dead. As numbness fell upon her, she cried out harshly and fell to her knees. Hospital staff paged the chaplain who assisted her with standing on her feet.

With tears rushing down her cheekbones, all should could hear was Mamie's words loud and clear.

"Baby I made it home. Go ahead and cry, but don't give up."

Walking to her car she searched for the strength to take it all in.

CHAPTER THREE

Passion passed the bar exam three weeks after her grandmother's funeral and was granted permission to practice law. A ceremony was being held for the graduating class at the Qwest Center in downtown Omaha. The whole Peckard Law and Associates firm was there to support their new partner. Tiara arrived making heads turn. Her dress was stunning. Tonight, Tiara decided to stay in the shadows as she watched Passion mingle with the crowd. It pleased her to see Passion come alive considering she had been in such a sad state lately. Tiara also knew that Passion was about to apply most of her time and energy towards her career. She observed how hectic and time consuming a lawyer's job could be, so she supported her friend one hundred percent.

After Passion acquainted herself with different lawyers and prosecutors, she brought two plates of food to the table and sat next to Tiara. They talked particularly about the salary which was starting off at ninety-four thousand dollars a year. Pretty good for an unproven rookie lawyer with a blank track record.

"That man is locking you in Passy. Gotta give it to old man Peckard he has a lot of sense honey. He knows exactly what he's doing," said Tiara.

"Yea Tee I'm fired up and ready to go. I'm a soldier I thought I told ya," rhymed Passion.

They both laughed, and fist pumped.

"Tiara, see most of these so-called lawyers are what you call green, they only look forward to receiving the check. They are puppets of the puppet masters, and will sell out their clients behind owed favors, you know what I mean? Instead of truly being down for the cause they're only interested in what they have to gain. See you may call them lawyers, but I consider myself to be more like an advocate."

"Ok so what's the difference Passy?"

"I'm glad you asked," smiled Passion. "An advocate shows absolute dedication to the client no matter what the situation is and will never let the adversary see us sweat. Didn't I just tell you I'm a soldier Tiara?"

"Ok well hold on Ms. Soldier. Watch this!"

Tiara smiled as she pulled out a pint of Peach Cîroc, and two shot glasses from her MK bag. Tiara held her shot glass in the air as Passion met her for the toast.

"Show them how it's done girlfriend!" said Tiara.

The ladies had a great time and finished off the evening riding the town listening to Power 106.9 on the radio. Shortly thereafter they called it a night. Passion needed plenty of rest since tomorrow was her first day on the job.

FIRST DAY

Passion confidently strutted through the halls of the
Douglas County Courthouse, eager to meet her first
client. His name was Terry Smith and due to his
charge of first degree murder, no bond was set. Terry
fired his first lawyer. There was something about him
that he couldn't quite place his finger on, but he also
observed his careless representation. Since he didn't
have the financial means to hire a lawyer, a public
defender was given to him. Passion pleaded with Mr.
Peckard to allow her to represent Mr. Smith. He
reluctantly agreed, although he was skeptical about
giving her such a huge case to start her career with.
He knew that Mr. Smith was going to take it to trial,
and the case would be a win-lose situation. Losses
didn't sit well with Mr. Peckard. Passion perused the
case file and felt more than confident enough that she
could win.

Twenty-four-year old Terry Smith, had allegedly
invaded his neighbor's home and shot him twice in the
head at point blank range. The homicide took place in
wee hours of the morning; however, the previous day
Terry and the victim Robert Johnson had a fist fight in
front of Terry's house. Neighbors saw the fight and
witnessed Terry get knocked out by the hands of
Robert who lived one block away from Terry.

 A neighbor to both parties, Leta Oliver said she saw
the fight, and observed Terry climbing into the window
of Roberts home minutes before she heard gunshots.
She was the prosecutor's key witness. Passion was

seated in the conference room looking over documents, when the door opened, and Terry entered into the courtroom. Passion stood up and waited as the deputy took his handcuffs off before she introduced herself.

"Hello Mr. Terry Smith, my name is Passion Veland. I've been assigned to represent your case."

"How long will you need with him Ms. Veland?" asked the deputy.

"Approximately twenty minutes' sir."

The deputy closed the door to give Passion and Terry their privacy.

"Mr. Smith, why did you fire your last lawyer?"

"I could tell he didn't care if an innocent man went to prison for the rest of his life. Do you?"

Passion looked him directly in his eyes.

"Yes Mr. Smith I care. Not only do I care, I take pride in my work and what I stand for, so let's get to the matter at hand."

Terry didn't expect that kind of response. He lightweight felt lucky.

"From my understanding they have already offered you a plea of twenty-five years and you declined is that correct?"

Terry nodded.

"Also, they have now reduced those years down to twenty and that's their final offer."

Terry gave it some thought with a worried look on his face.

"Coming home at forty-four doesn't seem so bad," he silently reasoned considering he was guilty as sin. "So, if I take it to trial and lose then what?"

"You probably wouldn't out live your release date."

Terry went back into contemplation mode.

"Do you believe you can help me beat this case?" Terry asked hopelessly.

"Yes Mr. Smith but let me say this, it is your life that's on trial here, so you have to do what's best for you. Trust me, I can reassure you that the prosecutor will need more evidence than what's been presented in order to beat us!"

His eyes widened.

"Not only are you pretty Ms. Veland, but you are definitely an angel. Yep let's take this bitch to trial."

The judge gave Passion one month to prepare for Terry's trial. Within that month she had other small cases that were less strenuous than Terry's until one morning when she came into work earlier than usual. A young lady was standing outside the firm at seven thirty in the morning.

"Hi, may I help you?" asked Passion.

"Yes, I'm looking to retain a lawyer and was referred to this place."

"Anyone in particular?"

"Well I was told everyone here was good. Are you a lawyer?"

"Yes, I am, and what did you say your name was?"

"Oh, I'm sorry my name is Jayme Thomas."

"Ok I'm Passion Veland nice to meet you."

The women shook hands then she followed Passion into her office.

"You can have a seat and I'll be right with you in just a second. Care for a cup of coffee or tea?"

"No thank you," replied Jayme.

Passion went into the kitchenette and made a pot of tea then back into the office. She sat down at her desk, lapped one leg over the other and took a deep breath.

"Ms. Thomas what brings you here?"

"My twin sister Mariah is being accused of killing her three-year-old daughter and I'm not buying it. She's a good mother and that is just something I believe my sister would not do," said Jayme with tears in her eyes.

"Ok now hold on Ms. Thomas there's no need to tear up honey and besides, it's too early for that kind of emotion in this office." They both smiled.

"I'm sorry," said Jayme.

"Well don't be sorry, I was just trying to make you smile. Listen Jayme, my concern isn't whether she's guilty or not, I deal strictly with evidence. Our firm has really great lawyers here that work extremely hard on our cases and it may be God's design for me to have met you first, however ten thousand is the minimum at this firm for a murder case. Will you be able to commit to that kind of financial obligation?"

"Yes, but I only have five thousand right now, but I'll do whatever's necessary to pay the rest."

"Well considering this case is in its early stages, I will allow you to pay half now and you can close out the rest in payments, how does that sound?"

"Blessed!" said Jayme.

She removed an envelope with five thousand dollars from her coat pocket and handed it to Passion.

"First things first, I will need to make a copy of your identification. Going forward I will start by obtaining her case documents to see exactly what they have on her. Here's a pen and paper, write down a number where I can get a hold of you when I need you. Rest assured Jayme your sister is in good hands."

****

This Mariah Thomas case was high profile and once again Mr. Peckard was reluctant about Passion handling such a case.

"Mr. Peckard, I don't need training wheels here, I need your support. Now I know I'm considered a rookie, but I'm as ready as any lawyer here. Please allow me to show you that sir."

Mr. Peckard paused and shook his head with a smile.

"Okay Passion, your wish is granted, but promise me that if you need any advice, an opinion, or assistance, you will come to me!"

"I promise sir!"

She grinned and gave Mr. Peckard a tight hug.

When Passion went to the county jail to visit Mariah, she was updated about every detail of the case. Mariah had left her daughter in the house asleep while she made a quick run to the corner store down the street. Within 15 minutes her house was burglarized, and her daughter was strangled to death. Upon returning home she found her three-year-old daughter's lifeless body sprawled out on the floor. Immediately she called the police. Two days later Mariah was arrested for the murder. Police had evidence that Mariah had called the child's father threatening to kill their daughter prior to her death. Frank Johnson stated that Mariah called him crying all week threatening to kill their child if he didn't come back to her. Coincidentally that very same week their child was dead.

By the time Passion read this information the correctional guard signaled that Mariah was ready for the visit.

Separated by plexiglass, Passion sat down and put the phone to her ear. Mariah glared, rolled her eyes, and puckered up her lips at Passion when she sat down.

"Hello, my name is Passion Veland and I was retained by your sister Jayme."

"Yeah I know. I'm just wondering if hiring you was a smart idea," said Mariah.

"Well it's not a smart idea to have an attitude with me when I plan on fighting for your life now is it?"

Mariah absorbed her words and did away with the bad attitude.

"I'M NOT GUILTY!" Mariah sternly blurted.

"I don't care if you are guilty Ms. Thomas, my job is to save your life and that's what I intend to do! So, what I need for you to do right now is lower your tone!"

Passion stern words and serious demeanor caused her to tone down her voice.

"Are you really here for me or is it only about the money?" asked Mariah.

"Well I would be lying if I told you that money wasn't a factor, but money does not make me, I make the money. I am totally here for you, and I take pride in my job and what I stand for. Are you suggesting that you're taking this to trial?" asked Passion.

"I have no choice, I'm innocent."

"Well I will begin making my preparations and in the meantime what you need to do is stay strong in faith and allow me to handle the rest, how does that sound?" asked Passion.

"Like a beautiful plan Ms. Veland. Yes, beautiful indeed."

CHAPTER FOUR

Passion could tell Terry was nervous when he walked into the courtroom. Today was the first day of his trial, and although Passion refused to let it show, her nerves were getting the best of her. After the deputy removed his cuffs he sat down and looked into Passion's eyes and asked, "Am I doing the right thing?"

"Absolutely not! You're second guessing yourself at the wrong time. Now is the time to move forward Mr. Smith, there's no turning back." Passion replied sternly.

"You know what Ms. Veland, you right I'm tripping."

"We're about to select twelve jurors. The prosecutor will select six and you'll select six as well. Select the ones you think will be in your favor. Are you ready?" asked Passion.

Terry nodded yes.

"Well let's do it then!"

Jury selection was tedious and seemed unfavorable to him, considering all twelve jurors were white. Passion reassured Terry that color of skin was the least of his worries. The next day was opening arguments and Passions presentation was deeply elaborated. Nevertheless, Ms. Peterson (the prosecutor) was very sensible and demanding to say the least. Ms. Peterson called her first witness to the stand, Marquez Holley, a friend of the victim who had witnessed the fight take place. After he was sworn in, he sat down ready to testify.

"Mr. Holley do you see Terry Smith in this courtroom today?"

"Yes."

"Tell me what he is wearing and point him out."

"He is sitting right there wearing a white button up shirt and black slacks," replied Marquez while pointing in Terry's direction.

"Mr. Holley how long have you been a neighbor to the defendant?"

"For a long time."

"I need you to be more specific."

"About six years."

"If you could describe his character as you know him how would you describe it?"

"Very violent and intimidating," said Marquez.

"Can you remember an incident when he displayed violence other than the day of the fight?" the prosecutor asked.

"Objection your honor. That information is irrelevant to this case." Passion retorted.

The judge barked loud. "Overruled."

Passion bit her lower lip and sat back down after receiving her first petty defeat. Ms. Peterson smiled at the witness.

"Feel free to enlighten us about anything specific that you may remember Mr. Holley."

Marquez cleared his throat.

"I have a three-legged dog right now thanks to him."

"Him as in Terry Smith?" asked Ms. Peterson.

"Yes, he shot my dog in the leg."

"I object your honor!" Passion vehemently shouted.

"Explain to me your honor what does this have to do with the case?" Passion implored.

Ms. Peterson interjected.

"I'm simply underlining his violent behavioral patterns sir."

"Ms. Veland, I will only say this once, never ask a judge to explain again is that clear Ms. Veland?"

"I apologize sir."

"Thank you, now sit-down counsel!" yelled Judge Baker.

Passion reluctantly complied.

"Let's move forward Mr. Holley. Tell us about the fight between Robert Johnson and the defendant. What all did you observe on that particular day?" asked Ms. Peterson.

"I saw it all from my porch. Robert approached Terry and asked about the money that he owed him."

"Can you be more specific Mr. Holley."

"He said 'I need my money you owe me.' Terry then said, 'If you gone press me and be petty about it then you gone have to get it in blood."

"What happened after that?" Ms. Peterson asked.

"Robert punched him in the face and then they started boxing. Within a matter of seconds Robert gave him a one hitter quitter, which means he got knocked out with one good hit," said Marquez as he smiled.

"What did Robert do after he allegedly knocked out the defendant?"

"He walked down the street to his house."

"Okay please move forward and tell the court what happened next?"

"Terry woke up startled, jumped up and shouted. 'I'm gone kill that hoe ass nigga!' Terry went into his house and didn't come back out."

"No further questions your honor."

Passion slowly made her way to the witness stand and stared into Marquez eyes with her hands behind her back.

"First let me ask you about this dog situation since you made it relevant to this case. When your dog was shot, you took the animal to the veterinarian to receive further treatment is that correct?"

"Yep, I sure did."

"Did you file a police report on Terry Smith for allegedly shooting your dog?" asked Passion.

"No, but I didn't know until later on that day that he was the one who shot him."

"Hmm, I see, or maybe you were afraid to call the authorities because you're a drug dealer!"

"I object your honor!" Ms. Peterson yelled.

"Sustained. Ms. Veland that was a personal blow, do not, I repeat do not throw another one," Judge Baker said sternly.

Mr. Holley is currently out on bond at this very moment on a drug charge and the thought of that alone made Passion smile.

"How well do you know Mr. Terry Smith?" asked Passion.

"Well enough," Marquez replied sarcastically.

"That's not a good enough answer. Be more specific like you were regarding your dog Mr. Holley."

"We were good friends."

"In-laws to be exact. Terry fathered a child by your sister on your father's side, is that correct?"

"Yes," replied Marquez.

Passion paced slowly.

"So, let's start again. How well do you know Terry Smith?" asked Passion.

"I only know of him but never dealt with him like that."

"But you say he is violent and intimidating. Is it safe to say you are going off hearsay?" Passion questioned.

"Yes, and him shooting my dog!" Marquez angrily replied.

"Back to the dog again huh," Passion chuckled. "Let's move forward. Where exactly on the street did the fight take place?"

"In front of Terry's house."

"Exactly how far apart is your house from Terry's?"
"He paused for a brief second.

"About four houses down."

"Are they on the same side of the street or the opposite?"

"Opposite."

"Mr. Holley so you are stating to the courts that you actually heard word for word what was said between the two before Robert struck Terry?"

Marquez appeared confused and didn't quite understand where Passion was going with her questioning.

"In your earlier testimony you said you were on your porch. Let me remind you that you are under oath sir."

"They were super loud I heard it all," Marquez replied with a look of frustration.

"Your honor I have no further questions for this witness."

Mr. Peckard sat in the back extremely pleased with Passions cross examination. Passion made every witness that Ms. Peterson called to the stand seem unreliable. At the end of the day Passion tasted blood and Terry went back to his cell feeling hopeful.

Testimony continued on throughout the week. Ms. Peterson called her final witness to the stand. Fifty-two-year old Leta Oliver. Leta was sworn in and sat down. "How are you?" asked Ms. Peterson.

"I'm fine."

"How long have you stayed on Grant Street?"

"Well I'm a home owner and I've been there for about twenty-five years. Actually, twenty-five and a half years to be exact."

"Were you a friend of Mr. Robert Johnson?"

"No, we have no relation of any kind."

"What about Terry Smith, have you two had any dealings at all?" asked Ms. Peterson.

"No um we spoke, but that's about it."

"On the day of the fight, will you describe to the court what Terry was wearing?" Ms. Peterson asked.

"A red and yellow Lebron James Jersey with twenty-three on the front and back with some blue Levi's on."

"The same clothes he had on when he was fighting?" asked Ms. Peterson.

"Yes."

"Where were you when they were fighting?"

"I was on the opposite side of the street. I had just come from the store."

"Did you keep walking, or did you stay and watch?"

"Ms. Peterson I'm too old for that, I kept walking. I wasn't sure if bullets were about to start flying so I got out the way."

"I totally understand Ms. Oliver. What did you see at one thirty in the morning?"

"Well I was on the phone with my sister's Myla and Melissa. I got up to shut my bedroom window and saw a tall male figure with a Lebron James Jersey on walking on the side of Robert's house. I watched the man, but his back was turned to me. Although I didn't see his face I knew it was Terry. I saw him climb in the window, and the man didn't shatter any glass mind you, so I didn't call the police until after I heard the gunshots."

"Leta, can you estimate, about how far apart the gunshots were from the actual intrusion?"

"About three to three and a half minutes."

"Did you see him exit the house?"

"Well, for some odd reason I didn't, which was strange to me because I was watching the house the entire time until the police came."

"Maybe because the killer exited the backdoor and jumped the fence that's why you never saw an exit. Thank you for your time Ms. Oliver. I have no further questions your honor," Ms. Peterson concluded.

Passion stood as she took time to gather her thoughts.

"Ms. Oliver, at one thirty in the morning you alleged to have observed a male figure on the side of Robert's house but was unable to see his face. Is that correct?"

"Yes ma'am!"

"However, you say you know for a fact that this male is my client and that you could tell because of the Lebron James Jersey. Correct?"

Leta reluctantly nodded and replied yes with hesitation.

Passion turned and faced the jurors.

"Lebron James Jersey was the number one bestselling Jersey in America. Six thousand of that exact same color was sold in Nebraska the month of the victim's death." Passion turned back to Leta.

"You see Ms. Oliver. My client is clearly not the only one that owns a Lebron James Jersey, and definitely not the only tall male figure in this city either. Just because the killer wore the same Jersey my client wore earlier that day, does not make him the killer. I have no further questions your honor," said Passion.

Passions only witness was Terry's alibi, his girlfriend Zatina Hardnett, who testified that he was at her house at the time of the murder.

When Ms. Peterson cross examined Zatina she underlined the fact that she was a felon, to reduce her credibility. The testimony didn't take long. The trial lasted for a week before the closing arguments were presented.

Ms. Peterson took the floor.

"Ladies and gentlemen for eight days I have gone back and forth with Ms. Veland about a person who is obviously guilty for the murder of Robert Johnson.

They fought, he lost. Threatened to kill and was a man of his word. Yes, we know that jersey is famous, but let's be real here people, the odds are a million to one that someone else killed Mr. Robert Johnson, and the killer wore the same Jersey that Terry Smith was wearing. My witness did not have to see his face to know it was him. It's our responsibility as American people to exercise our rights in this court of law. To use our proper sense and make appropriate decisions in our courtrooms. When we do so, unconsciously, we save lives. We prevent these kinds of monsters from repeating these murderous acts that nine times out of ten will happen again if this man goes free. He killed once, he will kill again. If you all do your job today, another life will be saved tomorrow," concluded Ms. Peterson.

Passions adrenaline was pumping as she took the floor yet appeared to be calm and collected.

"First of all, a murder case must be tried properly. The evidence presented here today is based solely off hearsay and a considerably large amount of inconsistencies. There's absolutely no evidence linking him to the murder of Robert Johnson. We all agree they had a fight, but that doesn't mean he killed him. Allegedly the killer wore a Lebron James Jersey, but that does not link my client one way or another regardless of what he was wearing that day. Now Robert was friends with the witness Marquez Holley, a known drug dealer who is out on bond and testified here in court today. So now that we've established the fact that he was affiliated with drug dealers you must ask yourself, what kind of life was Mr. Johnson living?

To convict an innocent man is uglier than letting a guilty one walk. We literally have no evidence to convict Terry Smith therefore, I do not have to convince you all of his innocence. Proof has declared him innocent."

Passion finished her closing arguments with that last powerful statement.

Ms. Peterson final act of persuasion was heartfelt and deeply assimilated by the jurors as they left for deliberation. Two days passed, and a verdict was reached.

"Mr. Terry Smith will you please stand and face the jury?" asked Judge Baker.

"In the matter of the people of the state of Nebraska versus Terry Lance Smith case number B6544003 we the jury in the above entitled action find the defendant Terry Lance Smith not guilty of the crime of murder in violation of a felony upon Robert Johnson a human being as charged in count one."

Terry was stunned as he hugged Passion tightly with a wide smile. Ms. Peterson appeared frozen in her chair, unable to believe that a rookie lawyer had beat her. In her mind she had long ago admitted that Passion was good, but genuinely thought she had convinced the jurors that Terry Smith was guilty. She felt ashamed as she walked slowly to speak with Robert Johnson's family.

"Stay out of trouble," Passion told Terry as he was being ushered away. Peckard walked up and embraced Passion in his arms.

"You did an excellent job," smiled Mr. Peckard.

"You know I had to show off for my boss," Passion smiled wittingly.

"I think you developed an early nemesis."

Passion followed his eyes. Ms. Peterson was infuriated.

"She'll get over it," Passion shrugged her shoulders.

"Come on Passion, let's grab a bite to eat, I'm starved."

CHAPTER FIVE

Passion's victory was quickly spreading throughout the jurisdiction. Ms. Peterson was a tenacious prosecutor that suffered only a few losses throughout her career, so losing to a rookie was definitely good gossip for all her colleagues. Passion took it all in stride and didn't stay happy about her win for long. Instead of celebrating she remained humble and applied deep focus on the Mariah Thomas case. Passion decided to rent out a condo in west Omaha for concentration purposes and knew there was a possibility that Tiara may feel offended. She sat her down one night and had a talk with her about her plans.

"Tiara, I don't want you to take this the wrong way or feel as though I'm changing since I've passed the Bar, but I rented a condo in west Omaha. Listen, I really need to focus and rest as much as possible.

Tiara didn't like the thought of her moving out and wondered how their friendship would be going forward.

"Why do you have to move away Passy? You have always used the room upstairs as your office and I never bothered you while you are working. I mean why pay for another place? Besides I thought you had a piece of mind up there. I'll cook dinner and keep quiet as I always do. Loneliness can be a bitch sometimes and I'm used to you being here."

"I'm not moving to Africa. Matter of fact, I'll still be here a lot more than I'll be there. It's just that when

I'm upstairs working I know you're waiting on me to come to bed and I always feel compelled to turn in early. The condo is strictly for those nights when I need to apply deep focus to a case!".........

"Okay," Tiara reluctantly agreed. "Well can I have a key?"

"Why not? I have a key over here so that's only fair. Look at my little cry baby best friend. You need to stop acting like that." They both laughed.

"Girl, aint nobody gone leave you in the dust, stop worrying. You already know I've got to be on my shit Tiara!"

"Yeah your right Passy. I just hate change that's all."

"Is Shawn picking you up tonight?" asked Passion.

"Yeah in a couple of hours. Why, are you coming?" asked Tiara.

"Where are you guys going?"

"To his house. He claims he feels neglected by me."

"Now why would I want to come?"

"Passy you're always welcome and what's mines is yours, therefore he could be both of ours if you ever feel like fulfilling some type of secret fantasy," Tiara smirked.

"Girl Bye! Trust me Tee, he's all yours. Okay but hold on, now I'm wondering how long you've been holding this thought in." Passion was looking at Tiara and shaking her head at the same time.

"Girl that brain of yours be on one million. Bless your heart," Passion laughed out loud.

"Passion it's not funny, a threesome is a fantasy of mine." Tiara appeared frustrated.

"Well not mines Tiara! Look, I'm about to carry my tail to this shower girl and we're getting off this subject. GOOD DAY!" Passion rolled her eyes and walked away.

"Bitch," Tiara said quietly.

"I heard that you little freak," yelled Passion.

Tiara thought it would be zestful if all three of them would become lovers. She tried to shed the light on Passion, but she didn't bite. Although Tiara let it go for tonight, she had plans to change her mind sooner than later.

****

Mariah's case consumed most of Passions time and energy. She wondered if in fact she could beat this case, considering guilt was written all over it. First the threat against the father which was discovered to be true. Then the reckless decision to leave her child at home by herself. Close family and friends vouched for her character as a mother, stating she is caring and compassionate. Other than the threat, no further evidence pointed to her.

Mariah lived in a violent neighborhood where assault and burglaries happened frequently. Her house was burglarized a few years ago with verifiable public records. Passion used this source of information to her advantage in many ways, hoping it would overshadow Mariah's threat to kill her child.

On the other hand, the prosecutors did a hell of job trying to convince the jurors that Mariah was the murderer of her own child. Yet what appeared to be a convincing home run of a case for the prosecution, the favor remained on Mariah.

Mariah Thomas was found not guilty and miraculously Passion walked away victorious. Reporters and cameramen crowded her space as she made an exit from the courthouse. Passion was good at ignoring negative publicity until one tall scrawny white guy yelled out.

"Do you like getting monsters off, or are you just the devil's advocate?"

Passion stopped and looked the guy in his eyes and yelled, "I am not the devil's advocate, however, it's my job to defend my clients and I stand firm in my responsibility to do so. What you may consider guilty, I prove innocent."

CHAPTER SIX

The Mariah Thomas acquittal had shocked many, and within the blink of an eye Passion had become the people's first option at Peckards Law and Associates. Her career blossomed with each case. Most of her defendants that deserved heavy sentences either walked away with light jail time or an acquittal. All of her murder cases were found not guilty.

After eighteen months working at Peckards' firm, she decided it was now time to transition into her own. Mr. Peckard was in opposition, but there was nothing he could do or say to keep her. Destiny was calling, and the drive to see it through was on a full tank of gas. Veland's Law Firm consisted of a four-man team that included two lawyers and a secretary. Charlena Prescott and Ron Zawadski, were both in Passions' graduating class. Although they were eager to get the ball rolling with cases, Passion wanted to train them using her system of strategizing before sending them to the wolves. Not only was she the boss but a great teacher as well. It didn't take long for her leadership to pay off.

Passion was sitting in her office perusing over cases when a gentle knock on the door disturbed her thoughts.

"Come in." Bill Picalo stepped in the office with a steaming mug of tea in his hand.

"Thanks sweetie." She took the mug and sipped with caution.

"Looks like a full day in the courtroom for Ron and Charlene. I haven't seen them all day. Pro bono cases got their hands tied I guess," said Bill as he was trying to start a conversation. He ran his eyes up and down Passion and a moment of silence ensued. Bill, her secretary, was a forty-one-year old white guy who was married with no children. Nicely built but not what you would call a lady's man. Never been sexually involved with a black woman but ever since he started working for Passion, she'd become his undercover fantasy. Passion was the sexiest black woman he'd ever laid eyes on. She noticed his observation.

"Bill, how are you and the wife doing?"

"We're just fine. What made you ask boss?"

"Well considering the way you're ogling me, I thought maybe a divorce was at hand or something. Word of advice Bill, don't flirt with infidelity when you're married."

"Of course not," he replied. Bill quickly pivoted from her office which made Passion giggle in silence. She was tickled by the shy white guy staring with seduction is his eyes. All Passion could do was shake her head as he stumbled on his way out of her office.

Passion jumped right back into work mode and twenty minutes later she received a call from Bill.

"Excuse me Passion, but you have a visitor here to see you named Shawn Mattox."

"Send him back to my office in five minutes," replied Passion. Lately Tiara's boyfriend Shawn had been discreetly showing up at her trial events, scrutinizing her work ethic. He was amazed and highly impressed at how good she was. He knocked, and she welcomed him in. After he closed the door behind himself she gestured for him to have a seat while she continued speaking with a client on the phone. During her phone conversation, they locked eyes, but not in a sexual way. She had to admit he was a very handsome guy. Six feet three, wavy hair, smooth skin tone, with a nice build, that made her understand why her woman was also, his woman. Truthfully Passion didn't think Shawn cared for her considering she spent more time with Tiara then he did, but secretly he didn't mind. In fact, he knew they were lovers but pretended to be ignorant about it for reasons of his own.

Although he loved Tiara, time was of the essence and the streets had the majority of his. Nevertheless, he took care of Tiara faithfully and was happy that Passion kept her company the nights he was unavailable.

"Hey Shawn, what brings you here this morning?"

"Well you already know I've been watching you in action and let's just say I'm highly impressed."

"Why thank you Shawn!" replied Passion.

"I'll be thanking you in due time. Right now, I don't have any cases on my back, but preparation is everything. If you stay ready you don't have to get ready. You feel me!" He reached into his leather coat and pulled out twenty stacks. "I need a lawyer like you in my corner. Aint no telling what tomorrow may bring with the way I live."

"Ok Shawn, well as a new client of mine let me assure you that our communication is strictly confidential."

"That's good to know. So, is there anything I should sign?" asked Shawn.

"Yes, there is. Here is your receipt along with a confidentiality agreement, sign your John Doe and that's it!"

"Ok Passion I'll see you around."

"Ok Shawn enjoy the rest of your day."

A WEEK LATER

Passions' record was seven and zero handling murder cases and today was the beginning of another trial. Jason Ivory had allegedly shot his girlfriend to death. Although they didn't have the murder weapon, they had a witness that stated she witnessed the crime. He didn't have an alibi, but a gun powder residue test proved that he had fired a gun on the day of the murder. Passion still tried to work her magic by creating a false truth out of guilt, making an easy decision seem perplexing. Even though she did a great job, not even the Angels from heaven could save that man.

Jason was found guilty, and his case would never be forgotten. Passions' knees buckled as she experienced her first loss.

"I'm going to jail you ole stupid bitch! I THOUGHT YOU WAS WORTH SOMETHING! YOU AINT ABOUT SHIT!" Jason yelled. The defendant then tried to spit on Passion as he was ushered away. Passion didn't budge or yell back at the defendant, instead she remained in a trance like state, unable to believe that she'd actually lost this case. The courtroom was empty, as she slowly gathered her paperwork preparing to excuse herself from courtroom. Passion didn't realize that Ms. Peterson was observing her from across the room.

"Ms. Veland." Passion stopped abruptly. Ms. Peterson closed in on her. "As I look at you from across the room, I actually feel pity for you. Look at little miss I'll never lose Veland! I'm trying to figure out what made you think you were so special that you would never experience a loss.... Hello!"

"What makes you think you're special enough to receive an explanation?" replied Passion. Ms. Peterson smiled as she folded her arms.

"Look here bitch, the case spoke for itself. Now we're even and trust, this will not be my first time beating your black ass in this courtroom. Look at you, you can't win for losing." Ms. Peterson laughed out loud.

"Yes, laugh now and cry later, I'm prepared to face off with you every chance I get. You'll see just how special I am. Celebrate while you can because it will not happen again," Passion retorted.

"I'm shaking in my shoes," said Ms. Peterson.

"Listen lady I'm not the one to be fucked with. You're better off approaching one of these silver spoon whores, better yet Lucifer himself, before trying me. I don't know why I'm wasting my time talking to your dusty funny looking ass, bitch get to getting," stated Passion as she picked up her briefcase and stared at her dead in the eyes.

"Well, well, well. Little misses pretty Passion has her panties jumbled up. Yes, indeed my dear, I'm going celebrate your loss with a double shot of tequila on the rocks." Passion quickly walked towards the door. "Passion Veland!" yelled Mrs. Peterson. "Your intimidation game sucks just like your skills did in that last case. Passion slammed the door as she left the courtroom.

46

CHAPTER SEVEN

Passion walked into her condo and poured herself a tall glass of Earl Stevens. She was emotionally overwhelmed and felt defeated. Her thoughts juggled back and forth, trying to analyze what went wrong in the courtroom. Not only was she fearful of the possibility that losing could become a normality which would make her an average lawyer, but also mentally exhausted over her first loss.

Frustrated whenever the smile on that prosecutor's face would cross her mind, she decided to pour a second glass of wine. Feeling a tad bit tipsy she couldn't help but feel sad that she had fumbled her client's life.

"I cannot believe I allowed that scrawny, rot gut, greasy head tramp, win that case. GOT DAMN!" yelled Passion.

"Okay Passion, get yourself together girl. Just calm down," she whispered. The alcohol began to actuate. As she ruminated, ideas began to formulate. Her thoughts began to electrify her mind. All of sudden she sat up in the bed with a sly grin on her face.

She walked over to her file cabinet searching for two specific files. Terry Smith and Mariah Thomas. She sat on her living room floor Indian style perusing over their files as a plan devised in her mind.

It's been a while since she proved them innocent knowing they were guilty as sin. Pondering in her thoughts she grabbed her laptop searching for their phone numbers only to realize they were disconnected. Anxiety kicked in until she decided to look on Facebook and observed both profiles with phone numbers.

"Ah Ha, It's on now baby." Grabbing her cell phone, she quickly dialed Terry's number first. On the sixth ring a deep penetrating voice answered.

"Hello!" said Terry.

"Hello, may I speak with Terry Smith please?" Unfamiliar with her voice he hesitated to reply.

"This is him, who is this?"

"It shouldn't be that easy to forget the person that saved your life. This is the woman who convinced you to take your case to trial when you were in doubt." Suddenly Terry came alive.

"Damn, is this Passion Veland?"

"Yes indeed."

"I'm so glad to hear from you. I've been waiting for the chance to be able to express my appreciation for you saving my life. I consider you my guardian angel!" Suddenly he became wary of her call. "Wait a minute, is the case being picked up again or something?" He asked nervously. Passion chuckled.

"No, you're not in any trouble Terry. I'm calling you for a reason and the reason is very confidential. How about we meet to discuss a little business at your earliest convenience."

Terry's adrenaline started pumping at the idea of a rare opportunity.

"We can meet up tonight, just pick a time and place and I'll be there," said Terry. Passion looked at her wrist watch.

"How does the sports bar downtown on thirteenth and Dodge in one-hour sound?"

"Cool, I'll be there!"

"Ok Terry I'll see you there!"

After she hung up she called Mariah. To her surprise she answered on the first ring.

"Hello, may I speak with Mariah Thomas please?"

"Speaking."

"Hi Mariah, this is Passion Veland how are you doing today?"

"I'm good. Is there a problem or something?" Mariah asked quizzically.

"No, you're not in any trouble, actually I found your number on Facebook for reasons of my own."

"Can you tell me why?" asked Mariah.

"In time, but first I would like to meet with you face to face."

"Okay you can come to my house tomorrow around noon if that's a good time for you?"

"Yes, I'll see you then Mariah. Thank you!"

Passion grabbed her keys and headed to the sports bar. When she stepped into the bar, she noticed everyone's attention was on the eighty-inch television screen watching the Nebraska versus Ohio State football game. She visually scanned the place, but he wasn't there yet. After buying a bottle of Corona she found a table. Ten minutes later Terry warily entered the bar, immediately saw Passion, and headed her way. Passion stood as he approached.

"Hey there Terry. It's so good to see you." They briefly hugged.

"Passion now that I have the opportunity I would like to truly thank you for getting me off."

"No problem Terry that's what I do." They both sat down.

"Mr. Smith, how has life been treating you?"

"I guess I could complain but why. Hell, life is tough. Not to mention we have the government injecting Ebola and all kinds of other shit to control the damn population. Then the police done found a new hobby called 'Let's hunt' niggas.' Other than that, everything is copacetic!" Passion and Terry both giggled.

"Do I sense I'm sitting in front of a conspiracy theorist?" asked Passion.

50

"Nah I'm just talking shit!" Terry Smiled.

"Do you have any kids?" asked Passion.

"I have a daughter that is nine years old, but my baby mother uses her as a tool to hurt me, so I can't see her." Passion became sensitive to his response.

"You mean she doesn't allow you to spend time with her at all?"

"No ma'am, and it hurts but hey it's a long story, so we'd better cut to the chase. What was the reason for this meeting today cause I'm sure you're not looking for a boyfriend?"

"Ok I'm going to be straight up with you on my reason for being here Terry. I would like to hire you."

"Hire me to do what?" questioned Terry.

"To kill." Her candid reply had thrown him for a loop. He stared at her for a second.

"This is a joke, right? You want me to kill someone for you?"

"Well it's no one in particular, but whoever may be detrimental to a case I may be handling. Whether it's a witness, judge, prosecutor or cop it doesn't matter. Anyone who gets in my way," said Passion.

"Okay I see right now that you are serious as President Obama about this," said Terry.

"Good because I'm just as serious about this as I was when I was fighting for your life."

"Passion, I mean let's be real here, killing those kind of people is a far from easy task."

"I'll be your boss and will have access to all the information you'll need," said Passion. Terry gave it some thought.

"What's the pay like because I'm broke as hell!"

"Five thousand a job, but I can guarantee, it will get greater later." Terry was jobless, desperate, and hungry which made this opportunity feel like a blessing.

"I'm in Pas. Count me in this shit. Can I call you that?"

"Call me whatever you like but listen closely you may have a partner. I'll call you tomorrow to touch basis with you. I have to go meet with her first."

"Her?" asked Terry.

"Just trust my instincts okay?"

"You know what Pas, once again I'm putting my life in your hands. What about weapons, I guess I'm going to kill them with my looks right?"

Passion smiled. "Sooner than later I'm going to wire you some funds to buy what you need. Does ten thousand dollars sound feasible?"

"Damn you sure are serious girl and hell yeah that's more than enough!"

"Okay I'll keep in touch with you Terry, but in the mean-time, stay out the way."

"No doubt Pas!" After Passion left, Terry sat there stunned at what was just offered to him and was excited about making some money.

Mariah lived in the same house that was fake burglarized and the exact same place she killed her daughter. Passion didn't pull into the driveway she decided to park on the street. Ragged worn down homes aligned one another, and a few crack heads were out and about. As she made her way to the door she thought about Mariah's daughter being murdered and revulsion washed over her which made her dread going inside. Reluctantly she rang the doorbell.

Mariah was looking through her peephole, contemplating Passions visit. She waited and rang the doorbell once again. No answer. As Passion started walking towards her car, Mariah slowly opened up her door.

"Mariah, I thought you were gone. Is this a bad time?"

"No, it's not a bad time. I was in the basement washing clothes that's all. You can come in." Passion quickly observed the cheap old furniture, wandering roaches and peeling woodwork. Passion didn't pass judgment on her broken-down house, she just thought she was a monster for killing her daughter.

"Are you home alone?" asked Passion.

"Can't you tell?" Passion ignored the sarcastic remark.

"Mariah how are things going for you?"

Mariah chuckled. "How are things going? Look around lawyer, life is fucked up right now. To make matters worse my family think I really killed my daughter. After my sister retained you as my attorney and I won, she stopped speaking to me. I feel as though she thought I was going to be sent away for real. Wait, why am I telling you all of this. Why are you here Passion?"

"To help make things better," Passion replied. Mariah raised her eyebrows in surprise.

"You, help me?" Mariah twitched up her lips.

"Didn't I help save your life?" Mariah was silent. "I defended your life Mariah so why does me helping you once again sound strange?"

"What the hell do you want Passion? Coming over here out of the blue and think somebody is supposed to be jumping for joy. Get the fuck out of here with that bullshit," yelled Mariah.

"Maybe this is not a good idea after all. You don't seem like the kind of person for the job," said Passion. Mariah put her hands on her hips stubbornly.

"What kind of job?"

Passion headed towards the door.

"No wait Passion!" Mariah blocked her from leaving and became respectful. "Sorry for being rude, it's just been so hard for me lately. So please let's just start over because I can definitely use some work."

"This job is not legal honey. Would you still like to hear more?" asked Passion.

"Sure do," said Mariah.

"I've already hired one assassin, and if you agree, you will be his partner. Do you have the heart to kill Mariah?" asked Passion.

"I'll do whatever it takes to make a better life for myself. Rob, steal, whatever, but you need to elaborate more. How much you plan on paying me is the first question?"

"First of all, my goal is to become one of the top high-profile attorneys in the world. The more cases I win, equals a greater chance of me reaching my goal. My plans are to advocate for criminals all over America and becoming a first-choice lawyer. Just like how you are willing to do whatever it takes Mariah, so am I."

"You know what? Just like that I admire you for being willing to do whatever it takes. You're too pretty to do the dirty work, and that's understood. What I don't admire about you is that you're naive, which makes me nervous about doing business with you."

Passion was eager to hear her reasoning behind her statement.

"How do you know I'm not taping this conversation, so down the line I can bribe you? What if he and I, whoever the guy is, get caught up, do you trust us not to involve you? What if we freeze under pressure?" asked Mariah. Passion realized her weakness on the naive side. She wasn't thinking ahead of her devious ways and that alone could've caused problems, but she didn't waver in front of Mariah.

"I picked you two because I saw something in you when we met. Both incarcerated, fighting for your lives and refusing to take pleas, as well as resisting the system without believing you could win. Sometimes it's better to stand for what you believe in than to fall like a coward. Pride, perseverance, and patience are all beautiful qualities that most criminals aren't aware they possess, nevertheless that's why I'm here today Mariah."

"Picking me was the right decision, I feel you, but you have to promise me one thing though Passion. If I ever get into a jam will you take care of me while I'm in prison because I don't have anybody."

"If that were to happen, I promise until my dying days that you'll receive a healthy allowance." Mariah stuck out her hand, they shook hands.

"It isn't hard to kill but damn you haven't answered my question yet Passion. Stop playing!"

"I'm sorry Mariah what question?"

"What's that pay like?"

CHAPTER EIGHT

Passion made a nice Sunday dinner at her condo for her two newly hired employees, Terry and Mariah. Their acquaintance seemed awkward at first but after a few sips of Christian Brothers their moods became luminous. Passion observed their chemistry as they all ate and talked at the dinner table. Mariah was talkative, and Terry was laid back, yet he slowly included himself in the conversation. After Terry was done eating he reached into his pocket.

"Mind if I roll up?" asked Terry.

"HELL NO TERRY! First of all, you are not allowed to smoke that reefer in my home. Are you serious! Secondly, how often do you get high because we do not need that habit to interfere with what we have going on." Passion frowned and rolled her eyes.

"Yes, she does have a strong point Terry." Mariah added.

"Passion don't trip man I got this." Terry smiled. Passion cut him off.

"Don't trip huh! Look this is some serious shit we're about to partake in. We don't need your habit to cause any mishaps."

"It won't Pas damn I hate I even asked that question. My bad damn." Terry pouted. That tickled Passion.

"Did you buy some guns?" asked Passion.

"We have everything we need Pas. I hit up my guy in Kansas City. He provided everything for a smooth

playa's price," Terry said as he smiled. Passion figured Terry probably kept some of the money for himself considering he came over with the latest Jordan sneakers on. She didn't mind as long as he purchased what they needed for the job.

"When is our first assignment?" asked Mariah.

"Be patient guys! Now of course we hardly know one another on a personal level, but we must be a team. Trust and loyalty are two factors that must be established amongst us. How can I trust you guys to not involve me if things were to go wrong?" said Passion with a serious look on her face.

Terry commented, "First of all, I'm far from a snitch. Yea I know just by me telling you this is not convincing, but I'm not. I would never want to look at myself in the mirror and be disappointed at what I see. I could be doing one hundred years as long as my integrity is doing it with me. I want no regrets. Passion listen to me. When a man has lost his integrity, I reckon his spirit will lose zest as well. I vowed to never become that guy."

"Amen," Mariah cosigned.

"Well my instincts tell me to believe in the both of you guys. Therefore, I will trust you two with my life. In return, I need you two to trust me with yours. Terry if things didn't work out and you went to jail for a long time, what could I possibly do to help you maintain mentally?"

Terry paused and gave it some thought. "Besides putting money on my books every month, you can look out for my mother. She's diabetic and we don't have the kind of income that provides her with the medicine and insulin that she need."

"She doesn't have the insulin that she needs now at this moment?" asked Passion.

"Nah."

"Well Terry let's not wait for a mishap to occur. I'll start paying for her insulin immediately."

"Are you serious?" asked Terry.

"Serious as I were when I saved your life."

Passion gave Mariah her attention. "Besides me looking out for your books, what could I do to help you maintain as well?"

"Passion like I told you before, my family has disowned me since the death of my daughter. They believe I'm guilty and so I've learned to respect their beliefs. So basically, I don't have anyone in my corner. Then suddenly you came along with a way to help me financially and I respect you for that. Just be a friend okay, because you definitely will have a friend in me."

****

Shawn and his supplier Shakeem had become closer than close over the years. It was no longer about business between them they were like brothers. Shakeem's daughter called Shawn 'Uncle Shawn,' and whenever he was around, his baby mother Malaysia considered Shawn to be a true friend of the family.

Shakeem had a wife, and although their marriage failed they didn't divorce and remained close friends.

Shawn rung Malaysia's doorbell while scanning the scenery. Light had just transformed to night and the quiet suburban street appeared deserted.

"Who is it?" asked Malaysia disturbed by the consecutive ringing of her doorbell.

"Malaysia it's me Shawn open the door! Shakeem was in a serious accident and is fighting for his life." She frantically opened the door.

"Shawn oh my goodness what happened?" she asked with tears in her eyes. Shakeem's daughter Candace was lying on the sofa.

"Hey uncle Shawn, what's wrong?"

"Your dad was in a car accident and is in the hospital."

"How serious was it?" Malaysia's voice quivered. "Go get your coat baby. HURRY UP!" Malaysia yelled as she quickly turned around and headed towards the upstairs.

She never saw it coming. A gunshot to the back of her head at point blank range ended her life. Candace froze in her tracks as she witnessed her mother bleeding to death. She turned and ran until a bullet knocked her off her feet. Candace laid still.

Shawn knew like always the drugs would sit at Malaysia's house for a couple of days untouched before he made preparations. After watching and studying Shakeem over the last couple of years, he finally picked tonight to make a move. A garbage bag full of kilos awaited him in the basement. He grabbed the bag and quietly made his exit from the back door of the house. A pair of eyes watched him as he walked off down the street with his skull cap pulled low.

Candace slowly crawled to the phone and dialed nine one-one. A dispatcher answered. "Nine one-one. What's your emergency?"

"My mother was shot, and I think she's dead and I think I'm dying too please help us. My Uncle Shawn did it."

"Hello, HELLO!" yelled the dispatcher. "What is your address honey? Help is on the way. Are you there? Are you there?"

No answer from Candace as she laid there bleeding profusely from her wound. The dispatcher closed her eyes and said a prayer due to the chills that ran through her body hearing this young girl's plea. When the police arrived at the bloody scene they were both pronounced dead. A nearby neighbor that was warming up his car at the time stated he had laid eyes on Shawn as he left Malaysia's home. He observed him walking down the street with a bag and didn't think nothing of it. When he returned home an hour later, the road was blocked off and the police had swarmed the entire neighborhood. After he heard the story from another neighbor standing nearby, he was willing to help anyway he could, and would soon become an important witness to this case.

Two days later Shawn was a murder suspect and wanted for the enormity crimes he had committed. Tiara had not heard from Shawn in a couple of days and was deeply worried about the situation. Word spread fast throughout the city and it didn't take long for people to start chattering about the murders. Passion knew it was only a matter of time before he was arrested and her duty to defend him was at hand.

Shakeem shook the streets down searching for Shawn but was unable to find him. Discombobulated with the harsh feeling of regret and overwhelmed with sadness and grief, he took his own life.

After a month on the run, Shawn turned himself in. No questions were answered until he spoke with Passion. She aided him in no time and instructed him to remain silent. He was in total compliance.

"Passion tell my baby that I'm innocent and convince her that everything is going to be okay. Also tell her to go to my mother's house and pick up the package I left her. She should be straight with twenty stacks until I get out of this mess."

"She will be straight regardless, but I will deliver the message." Passion assured him.

****

Terry was in his basement getting his workout in as his daughter pervaded his thoughts. The more he thought about her, the harder he worked out to relieve his stress, which had become a habit ever since he was denied his parental rights.

Her name was Evelyn. Nine years old and she considered her stepfather Ronnie to be her father. Ten years ago, Terry and Mildred were a couple until infidelity on Terry's behalf broke them apart. While Mildred was pregnant with Evelyn she found out Terry had sex with her cousin, and bitterness pushed her away. Mildred allowed him to come around Evelyn the first few years of her life, then she fell in love with a guy that was very possessive. Ronnie wanted to adopt Evelyn and felt that Terry's presence would no longer be needed.

Mildred met Terry at a public park and tenaciously established an agreement.

"Terry as you know, I'm about to get married to Ronnie. We're a happy family. I'm sure you would like to be present and supportive with what you can earn from time to time, but you don't have to worry anymore. Save your money. There's no need to buy her anything and child support will never be a problem for you. I just want you to move on with your life and allow Evelyn to love Ronnie as she is doing." Terry couldn't believe the audacity of her.

"What the fuck do you mean Mildred? That's my daughter and I love her to death. I'm not about to give her away to another man. ARE YOU FUCKING INSANE?" yelled Terry.

"Look, I'm coming at you nicely. So stop yelling at me Terry! Don't make this situation get ugly. I will fill her head up with so much negativity about you that she will hate your ass. Furthermore, I will move to another state if need be. Try me!" Mildred threatened. "Remember Terry, you did this to yourself. You created this situation!"

Terry felt hopeless, as he got up and left without another word. That night he contemplated this situation, and realized he had no choice but to let this go for the sake of his three-year-old daughter. He didn't want to take her through turmoil and confusion. He promised himself that he would regain his relationship with her when she was much older, so he could fully explain to her why he wasn't around. It was now six years later, and he had become a total stranger to his daughter.

CHAPTER NINE

Terry did his final set of pull ups and headed for the shower. After getting dressed he climbed into his seventy-nine Monte Carlo that was barely surviving the winter. As he waited for his car to warm up he analyzed his life and what it had amounted to. Ever since relinquishing his fatherly duties, he became violent and reckless. Off and on drug dealer, shot a few people, killed a guy, snorted heroin occasionally, and now a hired assassin.

"Where in the hell am I going in this lifetime?" he questioned himself as he backed out of his driveway and pulled off. As he drove by Evelyn's house, to his surprise, there she was sitting in the yard building a snowman. He circled the block a few times then parked a few houses down as he had done on many occasions. Today as he watched his daughter he hated himself for allowing Mildred to dictate such a valuable loss in his life. His resemblance was deeply etched in her features and he smiled at how beautiful she had become.

Ronnie pulled into the driveway and said something to Evelyn. He could tell she was ignoring him and stayed attentive to the snowman. Ronnie walked up to Evelyn observing her work and bent down waiting for a kiss. Evelyn reluctantly pecked him on the cheek. Terry balled up his fist as he continued to observe. Evelyn stood up and he pulled her close to his body. As they were walking up the stairs he discreetly dropped his hand and squeezed her buttocks before they entered the front door.

At first Terry thought his mind was playing tricks on him. He knew what he'd seen but didn't want to believe it. Once he decided to believe his eyes, his mind went blank. He started up his car and sharply pulled off to get home as soon as possible. He contemplated calling Mariah since they had just become partners, and realized he had no other choice.

"Mariah this is Terry, remember me?"

"Of course I do! What's up Terry?"

"You gone trip off this shit man. Are you busy today?" "Nah but it sounds to me like something is wrong. Is everything okay?"

"Listen Mariah I need to see you today before I hurt something!"

"Well, shit come get me!" replied Mariah. Terry wrote down her address and left the house. Before he went to pick up Mariah, he stopped by the dope house and picked up a gram of heroin and snorted in his car. By the time he arrived at her house he was numb, and his nerves were settled. Drugs made him feel as though he could think straight. Mariah was waiting at the front door and saw Terry pull up and made her way to his car.

"Hey partner what's up!" Mariah greeted him as he pulled away.

"It's all bad right now and I might need your help." Mariah could tell he was high.

"Before I ask you what for, what kind of weed was that because you look higher than Cooter Brown right about now!" He ignored her question.

"Mariah some serious shit is going on in my life right now and I may need you to help me straighten out this wrinkle," he said furiously.

"Okay relax a little bit and try telling me what's going on," Mariah amiably replied. Suddenly Terry became reticent. He had never elaborated on the situation about his personal life regarding his daughter with anyone. He now felt mortified about doing so and reluctantly told her the story. She listened and cursed Mildred a time or two but didn't interrupt until she received the entire story. When he finally finished, she could tell he was high on something other than weed, but right now it really didn't matter.

"Damn Terry! That is some deep shit. Wow! I'm feeling your pain right now man. What do you plan to do and what do you need me to do?" Mariah asked.

"First of all, murdering is about to become a hobby for us anyway, so we may as well make him our practice," Terry smiled.

"Fuck it. Sounds good to me, but when it's over, do you think you'll be able to see your daughter?" Terry was admiring Mariah more and more in a sisterly way.

"Although I feel like I'm behind in time with her, I have no other choice but to become her father again. That nigga will be out of the equation."

"Good thing is, you're not too late, so keep ya head up and let's get this perverted son of a bitch," said Mariah as she rolled her eyes.

Ronnie waited until Mildred was snoring and eased himself out of bed. As he crept across the room naked, grabbing his robe, he quietly made his way down the hall to Evelyn's room. It was three in the morning when he crept in like a stranger. Evelyn knew he would come into her room about this time, and the fear of that moment always kept her awake at night. After Ronnie molested her, it was then, she was able to fall asleep due to her silent tears and extreme fatigue both mentally and physically.

It started a few months ago while Mildred was at work. After he raped her, he promised to kill her and Mildred if she ever told anyone. Fearing he would fulfill his threat, she never told anyone, and accepted the abuse. All she could do was cry until he was finished. Evelyn started paying less attention to the teacher, who would often snap her out of reverie.

For recess she sat on the bench alone while the other kids ran around freely on the playground. "Hello Evelyn!" She turned around and faced him. Tears started to fall when he clearly observed the pain and sadness in her eyes. She didn't reply as she stared into his face.

"I know it may be hard for you to remember me, but if you think back far enough you will," said Terry. Her eyes began roaming over his face. "I'm your real father Evelyn, and you're my daughter. Remember when I used to pick you up and take you home with me. I would bring gifts to your house and tickle you until you almost laughed yourself into heaven. It's me baby, your dad." Slowly she nodded her head as if she slightly remembered, and Terry heart started pounding with joy.

"If you're my dad, why haven't I seen you in a long time? Are you sure you have the right kid?" she asked quizzically. That question punched Terry in the heart and a tear dropped from the corner of his eye.

"Baby I am one hundred percent sure. You used to call me daddy big head. I'm guessing because you thought my head was huge, and yes it still is." Evelyn giggled. "I'm your daddy baby." Evelyn wrapped her arms around him tight and they both cried silent tears.

"Why did you go away daddy, why? I needed you. I really, really needed you." Evelyn sobbed.

"I know baby I'm so sorry, and I promise from here on out to never leave you again. Are you okay? Is there anything bothering you? Is anyone hurting you? You can tell me anything." Suddenly a teacher approached.

"Excuse me sir but are you related to this child?"

"Yes, I'm her father!" Terry said sternly. The lady quickly saw the resemblance, but asked Evelyn anyway.

"Is that true darling?"

"Yes Mrs. Spencer that's my dad."

"I'll see you at home okay. Give daddy a hug." After they hugged affectionately, Mrs. Spencer grabbed her hand as Evelyn watched her father walk away.

****

Ronnie was a mechanic and worked inside the garage that was annexed to the gas station. Mariah watched from afar before deciding to enter.

"May I help you?" asked the receptionist.

"Hi, I was referred to a mechanic by the name of Ronnie. Is he available?"

"Right now, he's busy working on someone's vehicle, but I'll let him know you're here for service." The clerk started walking towards the garage unaware she was being followed. Ronnie and his partner were taking a cigarette break in the back of the garage. Mariah didn't know which one Ronnie was, but she intended to leave no witnesses behind. Both mechanics look perplexed about a customer coming into the work area.

"Excuse me miss but"..........

Mariah didn't allow the receptionist to finish as she swiftly pulled out a three fifty-seven from her coat pocket and shot the clerk dead in her face. Both men made a dash but had nowhere to run as Mariah was blocking the doorway.

"Which one of you child molesters is Ronnie?" she toyed. As they frantically pointed to the other one hiding their faces, she laughed making each bullet count, killing both men in cold blood. As she was exiting the gas station, a customer was headed inside.

She looked Mariah directly in the face and respectfully said hello as she passed her. Considering Mariah was wearing an old-fashioned wig with some big bifocals, she wasn't concerned. Mariah calmly walked over to the next block where the rental car awaited. Once inside the car she removed her wig and glasses and drove straight to her house as instructed.

Terry was worried about how Mariah handled her instruction, hoping everything went as planned. Instead of waiting for the outcome, he decided to head to Mildred's job. Wishing he could've killed Ronnie himself, he figured that going to her job would be a great alibi. He knew where Mildred and Ronnie worked from years of watching his daughter's whereabouts in silence. Every so often he'd follow them both home from work. He wanted to calculate how long it would take for them to arrive home, so he wouldn't blow his cover. At every red light his anger and anxiety increased. The thought of his daughter's pain and confusion tormented his very soul. Although he had no proof that Evelyn was being molested, what he had observed on that porch was convincing enough. Her silent cry for help alarmed him enough that he refused to allow his mind to tell him different.

Mildred was a registered nurse at Saint Joseph Hospital. Terry walked up to the nursing station and requested to speak with her regarding an important family matter. It was then that he saw the text message from Mariah that said, "done." He smiled inside but kept his poker face. When he observed Mildred step off the elevator he stood up as she approached the nursing station. The other nurse pointed him out. She hadn't seen Terry in years and slowly approached him with caution.

"Who told you I worked here Terry?"

"Listen Mildred we need to talk immediately, and this job is not the proper place. Let's step outside!" Something told her not to argue against what sounded like a direct order. She followed him outside.

"I cannot stay out here long Terry I have so much."........ Terry interjected and quickly spun around and pointed directly in her face.

"Bitch I could kill you dead right now. You better tell me right now that you had no idea what was going on with our daughter." His acrimonious words caught her off guard.

"Something is going on with Evelyn?" she curiously questioned.

He stared deeply in her eyes searching for the truth and found it. She didn't have any idea what was going on in her own home. He allowed himself to calm down before he went further by taking slow deep breaths in and out.

"Mildred, I have never stopped watching my daughter. The days she would play outside, I would be posted a couple houses down, praying for the day God will reunite us so I can be the father in her life that I should've been since day one. Since the day you and your perverted ass husband robbed me of my rights, I have beat myself up. What I saw the other day was very disturbing."

"Perverted! What did you see the other day and what in the hell are you talking about?" questioned Mildred.

"I'm talking about your lowdown ass husband grabbing my daughter's ass in a sexual manner that's what the fuck I'm talking about! After I saw that I went straight to her school to talk to her. I know she's afraid to tell on that man, but I saw her pain and to be totally honest, her eyes told me the truth. Your daughter, our daughter Evelyn is being molested!" Mildred could only stare at him as she was frozen by his words.

"Are you crazy Terry? I mean I know you're upset that I chose to exclude you from her life but that doesn't give you the right to come around my family trying to start shit. Especially some mess like this. See, this is the reason I kept your ass away. You're devious, manipulative, and your intentions were never good for no one, not even yourself.

"Ok Mildred fuck it. Let's go! Tell your boss you have a family emergency right now got dammit because we're going up to her school to find out the absolute truth. Let's see it at face value who's crazy in this situation. For one, I'll admit, maybe I'm part of the blame for allowing my rights to be stripped away, but I also blame you for not paying enough attention to your motherfucking daughter. Let's go!"

"Whatever Terry I'll be right back." Mildred went back into the hospital and explained to her boss that her daughter was at school with a high enough fever that she may need to see her doctor. Suddenly things were beginning to add up in Mildred's mind about Evelyn's behavior.

Her grades were slipping, and her personality had become hollow for some time now. She thought maybe she was experiencing puberty and often wondered how and when she was going to address her in a motherly way. Terry followed behind her trying hard not to let his anger cause him to speed. Arriving at the school, they both parked in a no parking zone anticipating this discussion at hand. Neither of them said a word as they waited on Evelyn to be brought into the office. Mildred was worried that his assumptions could be true, and she was dreading the outcome. Evelyn shyly entered into the office. Her eyes instantly became glued to her father as they stood up.

"Hi mom. Why are you off work so early?"

"Listen honey I need to have a talk with you. Go ahead and grab your coat so we can go home," said Mildred.

"Is daddy coming with us?"

Mildred was surprised that Evelyn called him daddy since she'd never explained to her who he really was.

"Yes baby I'm coming with you," he assured her as they left. Terry tailed them home. Mildred decided not to question her until they were all together. After they were in the house and seated, Mildred grabbed her daughter hand and looked sincerely into her innocent eyes.

"Evelyn, you know you can talk to mommy about anything right?" Evelyn nodded yes. Terry was observing carefully.

"Is there someone hurting you baby?" She hesitated and shook her head no. They could tell she was scared.

"Evelyn look at me," said Terry. She complied. "You don't have to be ashamed or scared because I'm not going to allow anything to happen to you again baby. I'm your real father and daddy big head loves you. I always have and always will. Tell us what is bothering you so we can help you. As your daddy I can look in your eyes and see that something is wrong." Evelyn observed the tears in her mother's eyes and started crying as well. Confessing between sobs and shaking, she revealed every detail, including the seed Ronnie planted threatening to kill anyone she told.

"Are you going to stay daddy? I don't want him to hurt us."

"I promise you here and now baby he is never going to hurt you again. How does your body feel? Does anything hurt on your body?" questioned Terry.

"I'm ok daddy, I'm just scared." The doorbell rang.

Mildred gathered herself as she answered the door staring dead in the eyes of two detectives. She stepped out closing the door behind her.

"How may I help you?"

"Hi ma'am. Are you the wife of Ronnie Palmers?"

"Yes I'm Mildred Palmers, is there a problem?"

"Mr. Palmers was murdered today at his jobsite. A triple homicide, him being one of the three. So we need to ask you a few questions."

The detective asked her several questions that took about fifteen minutes.'

After the detectives gave Mildred the third degree they left, and she nervously went back inside. Terry was talking with his daughter at the time she walked in.

"Did you do it?" she asked. "Evelyn go upstairs to your room while your father and I have a talk." She obediently went upstairs. Mildred was prepared to face off with Terry. Although she was upset with Ronnie, she didn't have the heart to wish death on him.

"That was the detectives at the door. He's been murdered, and it's mighty funny and strange.".........
Terry interrupted as he jumped up and closed in on her.

"Bitch look here, aint a damn thing funny or strange about nothing," he growled in a low tone. "You tried to take my daughter from me, and you should be dead with him." She covered her mouth as silent tears fell down her face. "Now I'm willing to forgive you for this only because you're her mother, but if you ever, EVER allow another one of your filthy niggas to stay under the same roof as my daughter again, so help me God I will kill you. Do you understand me loud and clear?" She skittishly nodded yes. She knew that he would fulfill that promise.

"From this day forward Mildred, I am vowing to be a part of her life. We will raise her together and this union will never be about us, only her." She nodded in agreement. "Remember, I do not want any niggas around my baby and if you think I killed that perverted sick bastard then go to the police with it. Let's see if they can prove it."

CHAPTER TEN

That night Terry went over to Mariah's house to catch up on lost time. She noticed he was abnormally high again but still gave him play by play of how the gas station plan unfolded. Scratchy with occasional nods told her that weed was not his drug of choice tonight. She hated the idea of him being hooked on anything else other than marijuana. The news came on and they intently tuned in. As the news reporter narrated the triple homicide, Mariah received an instant rush that would soon become an addiction. There were no leads, considering she had crossed paths with a customer as she was leaving.

"Job well done," said Terry after the story was over. "I appreciate your assistance today and I definitely owe you a favor."

"You don't owe me anything man. We're about to be involved in some heavy shit. I've just proved that I'm down for you and I believe you'll get the chance to prove that to me as well," she presumed. Although it was early, he felt like he could really trust her.

"Is she okay?" Mariah asked sounding concerned. Terry dropped his chin a few inches and briefly wept. Mariah attached herself to him and held him tight until he gathered himself. He wiped his face and began speaking in a tremulous tone.

"Physically she says she's okay, but mentally I know she is suffering inside."

"Then Terry, you'd better prepare yourself mentally to become her psychiatrist as well as her father. I believe you're an important factor in the way she heals inside,

but can you do that on the drugs is the question?"
Terry was surprised by her reply.

"What do you mean by that?"

"I mean you need to be at your best when dealing with her. Dammit cut the shit Terry it's obvious to me that you have a habit. Listen, now that you have re-established your position in her life, it's time to make some changes. You have got to get yourself together man."

"Okay Mariah I understand you, so don't start eating at a nigga preaching like your name is T.d. Fake, I mean T.d. Jake," Terry chuckled.

"That's funny. Well I just see you're emotionally all over the place so I'm just trying to be of some assistance that's all."

"Mariah don't mind me I'm just being goofy, and I know you mean well. It's just,"......Terry Paused with a sigh. "I've never expressed myself in front of a mere stranger before, just like I've never trusted a stranger. I guess it's a first time for everything." Mariah gave Terry a brotherly hug then stood up.

"Tighten up Terry don't forget we have to get rid of that gun man."

"Mariah you know what?"

"What?"

"You my nigga," smiled Terry.

****

Veland's Law firm was progressing at a fast pace. Handling cases was time consuming, but Passion's top priority. Balancing her time with Tiara had caused anxiety however she handled it the best way she could. Lately the Shawn Mattox case had most of her attention. With his pre-trial only a few weeks away, she spent countless hours in preparation mode. Although she was fully ready and prepared to battle this case in court, she also knew there was one small problem, Leonard Hines.

A twenty-seven-year old black man who saw Shawn leave Malaysia's premises around the time the murders took place. Mr. Hines was set to testify, and Passion knew that his testimony was critical to this case. Although she felt confident about beating the prosecutor's offense, witnesses always gave the prosecutor better odds and posed as a threat. So far in her career she has been almost flawless against breaking down the inconsistencies of the witness. Passion made up her mind that she had to put that last case behind her but wasn't about to allow Mr. Hines to dictate the outcome of this upcoming trial.

With Terry and Mariah's first mission at hand she arranged for them to meet her at the condo at nine o'clock p.m. A loud beep chirped through her office phone. It was her secretary Bill.

"Passion excuse me but you have a potential client here to see you by the name of Shantae Miles."

"Send her back Bill. Thank you."

Passion stood up as the door opened and welcomed a beautiful, tall, five feet nine conservatively dressed woman. Although she was beautiful, Passion quickly discerned that this lady wasn't dealing with a full deck of cards.

"Hi, May I help you?" asked Passion.

"May I have a seat?" asked Shantae.

"Of course. May I offer you a cup of coffee, tea, or bottled water?"

"No thank you Ms. Veland. Look let me get straight to the point of why I'm here is that ok Passion? May I call you Passion?"

"Yes you.".......Shantae interrupted.

"First of all, I'm the wife of Shakeem Miles. I believe you're defending the guy that killed his daughter, am I correct?"

"Why are you asking these questions Mrs. Miles, and yes, I am his lawyer, is there something you would like to add to this case that benefits my client, because if not then!!!...

Shantae interrupted.

"First of all, let me say this to you Passion and sorry for the interruption. That bastard buried Candace and her mother. Left them like garbage in a dumpster. Then my husband took his own life because he couldn't get over the fact that he allowed this monster to prey on his family and blamed himself. I will be in bereavement for the rest of my life behind the loss of my husband." Passion kept her poise sipping her tea as she leaned back in her chair.

"Look I know it's your job to defend criminals like Shawn, and from what I hear you're extremely good at what you do. Okay let me cut to the chase here. I'm offering you one hundred thousand dollars in cash to drop his case. If you agree, I'll deliver the money to you in cash first thing tomorrow morning."

Passion kept her composure but was really astounded from the boldness of this woman sitting in her office. She swallowed temptation to deviate from her integrity.

"Mrs. Miles, first of all, I'm sorry to hear about your loss and understand your reasoning behind this. However, you are sitting in front of a woman who takes pride in the work that she does. No amount of money could pay for the feeling I receive when I do my job and do it well. My honor is to defend every client to the best of my ability."

Passion sipped her tea.

"Not to be rude Mrs. Miles, but I have to get back to my workload for the day. I can walk you out or you are welcome to see yourself out. Hope you have a great day," smiled Passion. Shantae stood up with a sneaky grin on her face.

"Passion I wish we could've met on different circumstances, and all I can do at this point is respect your loyalty. Thank you for your time." Passion was surprised yet a tad bit disturbed watching her closely as she made her exit.

CHAPTER ELEVEN

Leonard Hines life consisted of early morning workout session's five days a week and working as a bartender at Lucky's Bar and Grill. Occasionally, he would deviate from his habitual flow of things and today was one of those days. Terry and Mariah began scoping his whereabouts several weeks in advance and decided that tonight was the perfect time to blowdown on Mr. Hines. Terry planned it all out and waited inside his home while Mariah was sent to follow him home from work. At exactly eleven forty-five Leonard locked the bar and headed towards his vehicle. Mariah scoped him close and heard him yelling at his cell phone but could not make out what his frustration was about. As he drove away Mariah discreetly trailed him on the freeway while dialing Terry's number.

"What's going on family?" Terry asked.

"I'm right behind him on the freeway, and he's not headed in your direction at all so what should I do?"

"Damn! Okay, look come back here and park a few houses down and let me know when he pulls up," Terry ordered.

"Sounds like a plan."

Mariah drove to her destination and parked. As she lit her Newport cigarette she became lost in a reverie like state. Reflecting on her only child Chrystal whom she killed 2 years ago. Chrystal was born mentally challenged and it troubled Mariah to see her in what she thought was a helpless situation.

Frank, Chrystal's father, became distant and his rueful actions became more apparent in Mariah's eyes. Soon their relationship was affected by their daughter's handicap and Mariah felt as though it was her daughter's fault that their relationship didn't survive.

Frank left Mariah for another woman and relinquished his role in his daughter's life as well. Mariah grew bitter and despised him for the pain he caused in her life which led to the demise of her very own child. Although she murdered her daughter, Mariah had convinced herself that her actions were justified. She felt as though she had freed her from the pain she would've suffered from this world. As time passed, guilt began to invade her thoughts daily. In the back of her mind she anticipated that God would punish her and always lived life feeling worthless. As she wiped the tears that began to fall all she could say was, "God please forgive me for killing Chrystal." Mariah quickly gathered herself and chain smoked her Newport's while waiting on Leonard to arrive.

Halfway through his shift Leonard received a call from his sister Keya crying hysterically.

"Butch is beating on mom again please go over there and see what's going on!" After calling his mother several times and getting her voicemail, all he could do was walk to his car yelling.

"This motherfucker got me fucked up. I'm sick of his raggedy, big belly, rusty foot, no good ass fucking with my mama!" Leonard rang the doorbell urgently.

"Who in the hell is ringing my doorbell like they pay bills up in this bitch?" Butch barked. Before Leonard could reply the door flung open. The two men glared at one another.

"What can I do for you at twelve fifteen in the morning man?" Leonard could smell alcohol as he observed the empty fifth of Jack Daniels sitting on the counter.

"Where's my mom Butch?"

"Nigga she's sleep where the fuck you think she is!"

"Look here man, I really don't want any trouble, I just need to make sure my mama is safe. Word got to me that you we're over here putting your hands on her and I asked you before to keep your hands in your pocket when you can't control your temper. 'Mamaaa Mamaaaa," Leonard yelled out.

"Look here boy ya mama is sleep. Now gone head on man she good."

"No, I need to see her face and all I'm saying is that if she has any bruises on her Butch, it's going to be a problem dude for real." Leonard pushed Butch out of the way and went back to the bedroom.

"Ma, are you ok?"

"Lenny baby I'm fine. Wait, did your sister call you, because I called her to confide in her and I was just a little sad tonight baby that's all. Nothing more, nothing less."

"Sad about what Ma?" Annie Jean turned around and Leonard spotted two purple marks on her neck that she was trying to hide. As tears instantly began to flow down the corners of his eyes, he pivoted towards the front door but was stopped abruptly by a thirty-eight-snub nose pointed directly to his forehead.

"Didn't I tell you she was ok little nigga? HUH!" Butch yelled as he poked the tip of the gun to his forehead.

"The only problem I'm gone have over here is where to dump your body the next time you step foot in my house on some bullshit, and it may not be a next time. I'm sick of you and your slow ass sister involving yourselves in what the fuck is going on over here. You know what? I should blow your got damn head off." Butch muttered. Leonard held his hands up.

"Look Butch you're what, six foot three, two hundred and thirty pounds. I'm six foot, one hundred and ninety pounds. How about you put that firearm away and show me how bad you are! A gun is a cowardly win and you would regret ya actions for the rest of your life." Butch sized him up then let out a loud beer burp in Leonard's face.

"Okay youngster, I guess you've never heard of these hands. Let's take it to the streets then. You're right I don't need no strap for ya ole scrawny Stebbie J on crack looking ass." Leonard marched his way to the street and waited for Butch.

While he was waiting on Butch he saw his mother following behind Butch yelling, "Don't go outside! That's my son Butch. He's only doing what a son who loves his mother would do. Keya is the one who called him! Please baby please. Go lay down honey, you're just tired." Butch pushed her out of the way which fueled Leonard's fire even more. As Butch walk towards him he observed another bruise on his mother's arm.

"Go in the house Annie Jean. He wants to challenge his elders, well I'm gone show him that age aint nothing but a number." As Butch drew closer,

Leonard attacked him with a jab and grab. Then he forcefully pushed Butch and followed up with a haymaker that made him do a fast cartwheel down the front lawn.

While he laid there appearing as though he was knocked out, Leonard yelled, "Mom go get a few things and let's go. You're not staying here tonight with this punk." As she stood astonished he grabbed her arms.

"Annie Jean, did you hear me! Let's get out of here," yelled Leonard.

He helped her grab a few items and then her keys and started walking towards the front door. All Leonard heard was his mother yelling, "Noooooo!!!" He turned around and saw the bullet fire running towards his face at point blank range. It killed him instantly. Then another shot was fired. It was Leonard's mother who was hit this time. Butch stood there staring at Leonard.

"You made me do this shit man, you forced my hand." He slowly walked to the ice box and grabbed a bottle of colt 45. He then turned on Al Green's greatest hits and closed his eyes while sobbing in silence. Butch had only been out of prison for two years after serving a twenty-three-year bit for murdering a man during a gas station robbery. As the reality of what he'd just done settled in with each passing moment, his thoughts began to race with confusion.

"After a full day of drinking Jack Daniels, and a twelve pack of Colt forty-five, this is how the night ended," he whispered.

Butch walked to the front door and looked around the room.

"I can't go back to that place. I'll never see the light of day again. Once again I allowed someone to make me lose my got damn mind." He picked up the empty bottle of Jack Daniels.

"All because of you Jack you dirty son of a bitch. Now look. My life is over because of you," Butch yelled out as he through the empty bottle of Jack across the room.

"My life is over. MY LIFE IS OFFICIALLY OVER!" He began to cry as he apologized to Annie Jean while grabbing a piece of paper and a pen.

"I'm saying sorry to all the people these deaths will affect. Just know I was sick. Alcohol was my religion. Please find it in your heart to forgive me. I am truly sorry." He grabbed his gun, looked at it, then stuffed the barrel in his mouth and pulled the trigger.

CHAPTER TWELVE

Shawn Trial was right around the corner and Passion desperately wanted Mr. Hines removed from this case. She found herself pacing the floors while staring at her cell phone several times throughout the morning.

"I can't believe they haven't called me yet." Frustrated and worried she decided to head out for an afternoon joyride to ease some of her anxiety. A few weeks ago, she purchased a brand new 2016 BMW X5. The weather was seventy-eight degrees with no wind.

"Oh yeah I may as well get cute, enjoy myself, and feed my new ride some speed," said Passion as she smiled while going through her closet.

"Ah ha! This blue and white 'LaQuan Smith' designed jean halter dress has been calling for me all month." Finishing it off with her white open toe Louboutin's and a few accessories, she headed out to her beamer. As soon as she turned the key, XM radio was playing her favorite song. Passion smiled as she nodded her head to the new Chris Brown record.

"I need a stiff drink right about now. See what you made me do C-breezy? You're about to have me all the way right!" Passion stopped at the neighborhood bar called, 'The Two.' Tiara normally hung there and assured Passion that it's upgraded and is now considered to be upscale.

"Wow seems like forever since I've been here, and it looks amazing! I'm so impressed! Double shot of Hennessy on the rocks please!" While gulping down the alcohol, she finally received a text message notification on her eye phone seven.

"What in the world is this?" she thought to herself. It was a link to the local news station.

"What's going on Terry?" Passion mumbled. "Breaking News, we now can release the names of the victims in the triple homicide we brought to you early this morning, located on sixtieth and Ames Avenue. Twenty-seven-year old Leonard Hines, sixty-two-year old Annie Jean Hines, and fifty-six-year old Butch Smith. Three bodies were found by the mail carrier as he observed the front door cracked open while trying to receive a signature for a certified letter delivery. At this time, we have no suspects in custody, however we will bring forth more information as we conduct our investigation."

Passion eyes were bulging as her heart began to race. "Damn, they killed three people!" She quickly grabbed her bag and dashed out to her car to call Terry. Before she could dial his number, an incoming call was coming in. It was Terry. Passion quickly answered.

"What happened Terry?"

"Listen Passion, the reason I sent that message before calling you was to let you know that we we're not responsible for what you've just read."

"As in, you guys never made that happen?" Passion said in a perplexed tone.

"Yes, that's exactly what I mean. I would never tell you anything like that over the phone boss. Going forward keep that in mind. Okay woman!"

"I'm confused! So, you guys had nothing to do with it? Are you serious Terry because I don't play games when it comes down to business," asked Passion.

"Serious as Rick James in a dope house with six white blondes serious Passion," Terry giggled.

"Wow, yeah that's pretty damn serious then."

Terry and Passion both laughed out loud.

"Well enjoy your day and make sure you win that damn case!"

"Okay Terry, but you seriously need to find a way for you to inform me of a completed job. It felt like I was waiting forever. I was super nervous and felt like I almost caught a heart attack man. Whether the job was completed or not, I want to be the first one to know. Anything other than that is uncivilized. Is that clear mister?"

"You got it boss!"

THE FIRST DAY OF SHAWN'S TRIAL

Passion was prepared for whatever the prosecutor had under his sleeve. Forty-five-year old Brian Milano was one of the toughest in his jurisdiction. She knew that by him losing his primary witness, the ball would roll down her court. Although Brian knew that going into this case without Leonard would be challenging, he stood six foot three with his head held high and confident that factual evidence would work in his favor. Passion decided not to cross examine any of the prosecutor witnesses who were family members of the deceased. The primary reason for their testimony was to clarify how close Shakeem and Shawn were. Also, the prosecutor wanted the family members to explain how Shakeem's daughter addressed Shawn as her uncle.

Day two was tedious. The judge postponed the trial by one day due to an electrical outage. On the third day of trial Shakeem's wife Shantae took the stand. Passion carefully listened to her replies from the prosecutor questions.

"Do you see Shawn in this courtroom?"

"Yes," replied Shantae.

"Mrs. Miles, will you describe the closeness of Shakeem and Shawn's Friendship?" Passion stood up quickly.

"I object your honor. Her husband doesn't have anything to do with this trial."

Judge Faulkner turned to Brian.

"Is this essential to the case counsel?"

"Very!"

"Overruled. Continue on counsel."

"How dare you say my husband doesn't have anything to do with this trial!" Shantae yelled harshly. Brian asked the judge if he could have a private moment with his client.

"Yes, and make it briefly," replied Judge Faulkner.

"Mrs. Miles, I know this must be extremely hard for you. It takes courage and strength to come up here and look at the man whom we both know killed your husband, but for us to continue I need you to understand the character of this judge. Faulkner is tough. He will dismiss you from the courtroom if you cannot control your emotions. You have to stay level headed. Are you emotionally prepared to move forward?" Shantae wiped her tears and nodded yes.

"Describe your husbands' friendship with Shawn to the court," asked Brian.

"They were close and have been close for about four years now. He would often come over and eat dinner and when you saw Shakeem you saw Shawn as well."

"If you can exclude your knowledge about the nine one-one call, would you believe that Shawn Mattox

93

was behind these murders?" She didn't hesitate her answer.

"Him being a suspect didn't surprise me."

"Why is that Mrs. Miles?" asked Brian.

"Because my husband was a heavy drug dealer and he supplied Shawn. Since I didn't approve of him keeping drugs in our home, he would use Malaysia's place to stash his shipments."

The courtroom was extremely quiet as she revealed such information. Brian turned to the jurors.

"For the record the house in which the crime scene took place was in disarray, appearing as though someone was looking for something." Brian turned back to Shantae. "Mrs. Miles, did Shakeem say anything about Shawn days before the homicide?"

"Yes sir he sure did." Shantae paused and shook her head. "Three days before the homicide, we were in bed and I asked him what was wrong. He looked as if he had a lot on his mind. He said he was just thinking about how Shawn's been acting weird lately. He was contemplating cutting ties with him for a while. I didn't ask him anything else about it, because he'll withhold his thoughts from me If I ask too many questions. I was just happy he expressed himself at that moment."

"Do you know if your husband had any drugs at Malaysia's house at the time of the murders?"

"Yes he did."

"How accurate is that Mrs. Miles?"

"I'm one hundred percent sure. He told me the night before he died that he needed to go pick them up. I don't think he ever made it sir."

"Thank you, Mrs. Miles, I have no further questions your honor." Passion locked eyes with Mrs. Miles as she approached the stand and smiled briefly.

"Mrs. Miles, may I ask you to exclude the nine one-one call again and tell the court why it wouldn't be a surprise if Shawn was a suspect, considering their four-year brotherly friendship?" asked Passion. Shantae rolled her eyes.

"My husband sold weight and was the main supplier to Shawn so therefore I'm sure he had thoughts of robbing him, despite their friendship. That's how the game goes!" Passion nodded her head slowly.

"I see. So, you're telling the court that my client is a drug dealer as well as your deceased husband! Is that correct?"

"Yes, that's exactly what I'm saying."

"Neither my client or your husband has anything in public records solidifying or even indicating that they were ever involved with drugs."

"Well I guess they were lucky," Shantae blurted out sarcastically.

"Mrs. Miles are you fabricating a story to send my client to prison, condemning him behind the nine one-one call?"

"I object your honor! She is accusing the witness of lying!" Brian Shouted.

"Sustained, no more accusations Mrs. Veland."
Passion paced back and forth and abruptly stopped directly in front of Mrs. Miles.

"Did you, or did you not come into my office and offer me a large amount of money to drop Shawn's case?" Mrs. Miles became skittish. "I have it all on tape and please keep in mind that YOU ARE under oath Mrs. Miles."

"Yes I did," she reluctantly answered. Everyone in the courtroom appeared shocked.

"I wanted to make sure he got punished for what.........he ....did." She began to cry.

"Mrs. Miles since you were willing to pay me to drop my integrity, I have good reason to believe you will lie under oath. Especially in this matter."

"I'M NOT A LIAR," she shouted in tears.

"I have no further questions your honor." Passion took a seat.

As the trial continued to unfold, the prosecutor's evidence against Shawn had merely been reduced to surmising accusations. Brian Milano was now in a battle with Passion and her effusive examinations highlighted his worriment. The confidence that was once displayed at the beginning of trial was no longer apparent.

When the nine one-one tape was played, the courtroom listened quietly as Candace Miles attempted to reach out for help. Jurors gasped for air as they heard her voice turn silent which solidified her death. A few jurors were in tears after hearing the tape. Brian took the floor.

"You see ladies and gentlemen, with the absence of our primary witness, this tape clearly proves Mr. Mattox guilt. This eight-year-old child Candace Miles normally addressed him as uncle Shawn. In her attempt to seek help, she mumbled it was uncle Shawn. Family, friends, and the wife of the deceased testified that Shawn Mattox is the only man Candace called uncle Shawn. Now it is very unfortunate that they couldn't be here with us to testify, but I believe although Candace did not survive she fought for her last breath. She fought to stay alive in order to share the name of her killer. Ladies and gentlemen let's not cause her to turn over in her grave because justice did not prevail. A double homicide was committed and thanks to little Candace we know who committed this enormous act. Justice is at hand and today, Justice must.......be........served."

Passion confidently stood up once Brian took his seat. She slowly walked with a confident stride, pencil in hand tapping inside the other hand, and ready to proceed with her final arguments.

"February 28th was a sad day for the family of the deceased. As I genuinely extend my condolences, I also must keep in mind that I'm representing my client who is fighting for his life. My job here today was to prove to the court that without proper evidence, we must set this man free." Passion began to pace slowly giving the jurors eye contact. "Valid evidence, and non-valid evidence determines the outcome of a trial. Normally what happens when the prosecutor presents valid evidence against the defendant, the prosecutor wins the case, however ladies and gentlemen the evidence presented here today is shallow. Family members of the victims testified that in fact, Candace always addressed Mr. Mattox as uncle Shawn and is the only uncle Shawn that she knew. On the tape, yes it was clearly heard that Candace stated uncle Shawn did it, however let's take a deeper look inside what she said. If several family members were aware that Mr. Mattox was the only uncle Shawn she knew, imagine how many other people knew that as well. It leaves us no other choice but to ponder on the possibility that this could in fact be a set up! There's a huge possibility that whoever made her say uncle Shawn, could very well be someone with the intentions of throwing off the investigation. Could it have been a family member? Another business associate of Shakeem? I was offered one hundred grand to pull away from this case, which led me to believe even more so that my client was framed for these murders. Conjectures don't win cases, however non-valid evidence doesn't win favor either. Only Candace Miles could've told us if it was uncle Shawn, but one must ask. Was she forced to say that? This trial is based on inconclusive evidence and

a human life should not be at stake behind it. We cannot force justice upon the innocent, nor should we use our emotions to judge invalid evidence presented in this courtroom.
Today..........Justice......must.....................prevail.
Thank you!" Passion strutted with confidence as she concluded her closing statement.

It took three days for the jurors to deliberate and now Shawn's fate was in the hands of the judge. Passion stood next to her client unaware that her life was about to change. Yes, she expected and sought to become a prestigious lawyer one day but didn't realize that her dream would come true so quickly.

Shawn was found not guilty and acquitted on all charges. Although Shawn believed in her, he was still amazed that she was able to set him free. He hugged her tight and whispered in her ear, "How can I repay you for this?"

"No repayment needed Shawn just stay out of trouble. Tiara almost lost her mind without you," Passion smiled.

Shawn looked around the courtroom for Tiara. He spotted her crying tears of joy as she blew him a kiss before the deputy took him away.

CHAPTER THIRTEEN

Society along with members of the Douglas County jurisdiction were convinced without a doubt that Passion Veland was invincible. CNN covered bits and pieces of this story due to the trending and shared statuses on social media websites. Phone calls began to flow in as her clientele expanded from all around the globe. Prestigious clients with large bank accounts were retaining Passion just in case they needed her. Suddenly her career, law firm and lively hood invigorated tremendously. Passions workload didn't affect her relationship with Tiara.

Tiara understood that her nights spent at the condo meant Passion was applying focus to an upcoming trial.

Shawn, however was spending more time with Tiara since he was released. He wanted to show her that she was appreciated for the way she stood by his side while he was incarcerated. Tiara and Shawn were in bed together, and Shawn asked a surprising question.

"Baby I have a question, but I want you to be totally honest with me."

"Honest about what?" asked Tiara as she lifted her head from the pillow feeling nervous.

"Are you and ole girl Passion more than just friends? Or have I been just assuming over the years!" She laid her head on his chest and closed her eyes.

"If I tell you the truth Shawn will you promise not to hold it against me?"

"Umm, I guess, but dang babe you've basically just told on yourself," Shawn replied as he shook his head.

"Well the truth is, I love Passion and yes we had a situation years' ago and never detached. Does that make you feel some kind of way baby?"

"Nah, well, I mean it's shocking. Even though I knew it was true for real. Honestly I would only be upset if there were others besides me and Passion."

Tiara giggled. "No Bootskie there is no one else and let me assure you that I've never cheated on you with another man."

"Okay babe so tell me how it happened, you know you and Passions' first little episode or whatever."

"Well one night, a long time ago we were both lonely and it just happened and hasn't stopped."

"Do you like it better with her than me?"

"Wow! Why did I know that was the next question!" Tiara chuckled. "No way baby. Not at all. The both of you guys make me feel special in different ways. With Passion, I'm able to talk about things that of course you probably don't want to hear. With you, I feel safe, and of course you be fucking the shit out of me but that's the difference. I hope that by me talking to you about this doesn't change our relationship!"

Shawn respected her honesty and instantly began fantasizing about a threesome with Passion. He admired Passion's work ethic and calm persona, and after she exonerated him in court he developed secret feelings for her. Tiara observed Shawn in deep thought.

"What's on your mind handsome?"

"Nothing really babe. Just thinking that's all."

"Let me guess, you're thinking about how nice it would be to have all of us in the same bed huh?" Shawn's eyes got big and he grinned the widest smile Tiara has ever seen.

"How are you going to handle two beautiful women in the bed with you?"

"Okay Tee I'm not going to lie, I have been daydreaming about that lately."

"Well me too."

"I most definitely can handle the both of you don't get that twisted, but remember it has to be something that you really want!"

"Well of course I do! That's why I brought it up," said Tiara.

"Well, do you think Passion will go for it?" asked Shawn.

"Passion never took me serious when I brought it up a few times but how about we let her know just how serious we are babe. I have an idea," smiled Tiara.

****

Passion had been advocating in and out of town and although flying wasn't something she enjoyed, that soon became a normality. Once she got over daydreaming about the plane crashing, she actually started to relax and enjoy her flights. Today was her twenty-seventh birthday and already the sun was starting to hide. It was seven fifteen p.m. and to her surprise a taxi was available on the spot. On the ride to Tiaras' house, her mind began to reflect on the past.

This was the first time they hadn't made any plans for something special. Normally they would party from sundown to sunup, but she didn't want to believe that things were changing between them. Not to mention it felt as though the more her career blossomed, the more her sex drive decreased.

She promised Tiara she would start spending more time with her and thought her birthday would be the perfect day. Ding dong. Ding dong. Passion rang the doorbell and smiled as she saw Tiara open the front door. Tiara passed her a note.

"Hey Tee, what is this? Tiara what are you up to now. You're always up to something." Passion opened the note and read it while coming in the door. The note read: 'Grab the blindfold from the mailbox and put it on.'

After she put the blindfold on Tiara touched her mouth softly and whispered, "Don't talk just listen."

"Okay Jodeci, can you let me in on what trick you have up your sleeve?"

"Shush," said Tiara as she led Passion to the dining room table and sat her down. After she was seated she removed her blindfold and observed her favorite dish. Also, neatly placed was a bottle of wine floating on ice and rose petals in a heart shaped bowl. Passion covered her mouth as she observed the candles burning, chocolate covered strawberries and the sound of Kem playing in the background.

"Wow, all this for me? I'm totally captivated!" Tiara was wearing nothing but a robe. She opened the robe then sat on Passions lap and fed her a strawberry while her breast jiggled on Passion's lips.

"Okay now how about you eat while you catch me up to speed on how things been rolling for you lawyer lady," said Tiara.

"Really! You want me to eat after you just jiggled your boobies in my face huh! Well I guess I am starved. Thank you so much Tee I really appreciate this. My birthday turned out to be special after all. Let's turn up boo," Passion smiled.

As they sat and chatted about memories and moments in time, Tiara and Passion both exhaled.

"Passy are you ready for phase two?"

"Holy shit! There's more to come?" asked Passion.

"Of course! You've been working so hard lately you need this. On top of that it's your birthday."

"Well in that case, hell yeah!"

"Put your arms on my shoulders and let me guide you to the promise land," said Tiara. Passion chuckled as she followed her lead. Tiara had her Jacuzzi filled with bubbles and rose petals. Tiara undressed her, then grabbed her hands leading her into the tub. The ladies sat Indian style as they kissed and caressed one another's breast. They started to slow grind while Tiara whispered softly in her ear.

"I missed you baby," said Tiara while she blindfolded her again and led her out of the tub and into the bedroom. Passion laid on her back as Tiara caressed her body massaging her from head to toe. Soft touches and slow kisses had Passion quivering with every touch. Tiara began to lick her vagina slowly and touching her nipples at the same time causing Passion to grab Tiara by the face and kiss her passionately. Tiara slowly licked her from her neck down to her vagina as she started to massage her with her tongue. Passion was astonished and amazed by the special treatment she was receiving. While in the act Tiara motioned for Shawn to come join in as Passion remained blindfolded.

He tiptoed quietly to the bed and observed the two women make love. Shawn was in total bliss and his erection was starting to hurt. Tiara pulled back and stood up leaving Passion squirming and pleading for more. That's when Shawn got in between Passions legs and started tasting her clitoris. She didn't recognize the switch and loved every single minute of it. After he felt her have an orgasm on his tongue, he stopped and inserted his penis inside her. Before she could pull the blindfold off, Tiara penned her arms to the bed. Passion screamed and cursed at Shawn as he dug inside her deeper and deeper.

"Baby, relax it's your birthday don't fight it. Let's enjoy this together," said Tiara. At that moment Passion knew that Tiara was living out her fantasy. Although she was upset that Tiara set this up, she decided to give into the moment as she was being forced to do so anyway. While Shawn was stroking her slowly Tiara began to caress her nipples. Passion had never experienced the sensation of a man inside her, but to her surprise this felt better than she expected. Passion started giving it back to him, throwing her vagina up in the air onto his penis meeting him in the middle.

Passion thought since Tiara started something, she may as well finish it. She enkindled the moment.

"Yes, daddy fuck me! Fuck this pussy. Oh, Shawn you feel so damn good. Just take it all baby, take me." Passion started moving in a circular motion with Shawn as he massaged his penis inside her deeper and deeper. He felt like a champion, especially since she was still wearing the blindfold but assumed it was him.

"Pas you are making me cum girl! This pussy is so tight and wet on this dick." Passion began to have an orgasm as she clawed his back while moaning and groaning at the same time.

"Cum all over this pussy Shawn. Yes! I love it. It feels so good," Passion moaned. Tiara stood there and watched them both cum at the same time. Shawn laid on top of Passion cuddled as the sensation paralyzed his movement. They both had their arms wrapped around each other tight as if they were holding on for dear life. Tiara was lying next to them with a tad bit of jealousy flowing through her veins and was eager to break up the closeness she was observing.

"Shawn! Let's go grab some food in the kitchen for all of us," said Tiara. Her and Shawn walked into the kitchen.

Passion laid in bed in awe. She couldn't believe what had just happened and her emotions were all over the place. Feeling a sense of betrayal and deception yet enjoying the feeling of a man making love to her. She removed her blindfold and went straight to the bathroom to soak in the tub. Fifteen minutes later Tiara came in the bathroom and sat on the edge of the tub.

"Before you say anything Pas, just hear me out okay. I thought this would be a birthday to remember. A new experience as well as some fresh excitement that neither one of us had yet to experience." Passion interrupted.

"First of all, do you have any idea what just happened?"

"Yes, I mean"........ Passion interrupted her again.

"You allowed your boyfriend to rape me." Tiara didn't reply realizing that her plan had just backfired. "It was all about you once again. Everything is always about you." Tears began to flow down Passion's face. "This was your fantasy and betraying my trust is how you could make this happen? What you need to realize is that this situation is far from simplistic. Oh no honey. See we can't just throw this one under the rug!" Passion shook her head. "Well Tee, you got what you wanted. You lived out your dirty little fantasy and you know what? I really hope it was worth our friendship because I am so done with you. The killer part is, your thirsty ass held me down and everything. That's crazy as shit Tiara!" Tiara touched Passions hands.

"Baby I love you so much. You're my world Pas and I can't live without you. Please don't leave Pas, I just,"............... Passion snatched her hands back.

"Bitch don't touch me! You deceived me in the worst way," yelled Passion.

"Pas I didn't think you would be so upset like this. I just wanted to add spice in our relationship. That's all."

"By me being raped? Really? asked Passion.

"Well damn Pas forgive me for saying this but it looked as though the two of you were starting to bond a little bit. I mean you guys held each other at the end, so it wasn't all that bad. Damn! If it was, I damn sure couldn't tell." Passion looked at Tiara with fire in her eyes.

"So that's all you have to say about that huh. Yeah and I hope that memory remains in your tiny little brain every time you lay in bed with him and guess what Tiara? That dick felt damn good. I didn't know dick could make this thang do all of what it just did. Maybe I'll keep fucking him. What's good for the goose is good for the gander," yelled Passion.

Tiara began to cry as Passion gathered her items and went for the door. Passion stopped and looked her square in her eyes.

"Oh, the thought of that brought tears to them little evil eyes huh," Passion chuckled. "Girl bye! Don't call my damn phone crying and shit because I don't want to hear nothing you have to say." Before Passion left she observed Shawn sitting on the couch with his head held down. She made eye contact with him, smiled, and shook her head. Without saying another word, she gave them both the middle finger and slammed the door.

CHAPTER FOURTEEN

Passion remained unforgiving toward Tiara as weeks passed. Refusing to return any text messages or listen to the twenty plus voicemails that flooded her inbox. There was no way Passion could ever trust her again and she resolutely accepted her decision.

Passion and her two lawyers, Charlena Prescott and Ron Zawadski were seated in her office. The meeting consisted of teaching tactical lessons to apply into their defense. They both sat eager to learn from their boss whom was now labeled one of the top ten greatest female attorney's in the nation. They were abruptly interrupted by a call from the receptionist.

"You have a visitor here to see you. He says his name is Shawn Mattox," stated Bill. Passion was private when it pertained to her personal business, and he was the last person she wanted to see.

"Send him in." Ron and Charlena walked out as Shawn walked in and closed the door behind himself. Passion sat back in her chair and looked at him but didn't say a word.

"How are you Passion? You mind if I sit in one of these fancy chairs?"

"Be my guest," said Passion. They stared at one another for a moment.

"Passion I'm here on Tiara's behalf. She didn't expect this to happen. You know......you being so upset and all. Shawn stuttered his words as his nervousness got the best of him. "Her hopes was that the situation would bring all three of us together. That's all," said Shawn.

"The three of us together huh? Are you kidding me. Okay hold up. Let's dissect what you just said. By you and her raping me, togetherness was the ulterior motive? You have got to be kidding me," said Passion as shook her head and laughed out loud. "Look I really don't know what to tell you Shawn I'm still angry as if it happened today. I feel violated and I just don't....... Shawn interrupted.

"Passion, I'm just gone keep it all the way one hundred with you. I didn't come here for Tiara. Our experience was breathtaking. Being inside you was a feeling like never before and I felt connected to you in a way I really can't explain. I dream about you every night, and not to mention you saved my life. So, the feelings I hold on to when it comes to you is personal and far from business. Truthfully, I don't even care how Tiara feel about it. I'm sorry, it is what it is," Shawn grinned, showing them pearl white teeth.

Passion didn't expect this kind of reaction from him, nevertheless she never interrupted his effusive approach.

"Check this out Passion If I knew you had no clue of what was about to happen, I would've never agreed to participate. I'm far from a rapist shorty. Trust me, I was under the wrong impression." Shawn lied hoping to win favor.

"So, she lied to the both of us then. Hmm that Tiara is a motherfucker," smiled Passion.

"Look doe Passion baby, I don't want to damage your relationship with her. All I want from you is a chance to be able to see you again. I really would love that," smiled Shawn.

"Get out of my office Shawn this is my place of business." Shawn chuckled and stood up.

"Calm down sexy! I mean, I understand your reason for being highly upset, but don't direct that towards me doe. Aight! I'll see you around."

After he left she sat back and contemplated his visit. Memories of the way he felt inside her made her panties moist and she desperately tried to deny the late-night cravings for his body inside of her. Up until that moment her whole sex life revolved around Tiara. Other than the two close calls in college, this was her first real experience of a man inside her. Unsure of how she should identify with her new-found man desires, she tried to block it out her mind, but her body told her otherwise. All she knew was that she wanted him more and more and more.

MOVING ALONG

The famous three time (pro-bowl) wide receiver for the Oakland Raiders, Omar Massingil was booked and charged for the murders of his ex-wife and her new husband. Every news station and sports channel on television was showing footage of him in handcuffs. America was shocked and in disbelief. Omar was loved by so many people who refused to believe that these allegations were true. His wife retained Passion one day after he was arrested. Passion immediately caught a flight out to Oakland to visit him in jail. Although she was a huge fan, she felt saddened that she had to greet him this way. As she watched Omar ingress into the visitation room, she could tell he was nervous. Money, fame, and fortune were once the most important highlights of his life and now all of that seemed mediocre compared to what he was up against. Passion however considered nervousness as a sign of guilt, but her only concern was winning the case. Omar sat down and put the phone to his ear.

"Hi Omar. My name is Passion Veland." Passion cleared her throat. "I was retained by your wife yesterday. First things first. Have you spoke with any other officials regarding this case other than myself today sir?"

"Well first of all, I want to say thank you for taking my case and no I haven't spoken to anyone about anything. It's ironic! Me meeting you this way because I had just told my agent, well last year, that if I was to ever get myself into a bind, to retain you as my lawyer. I've always been amazed by your work, but I never thought I would need your services and especially for something like this. All I know is that I'm innocent." Omar held his head down with tears in his eyes.

"I understand Omar and my job and goal is to win this case, so pick your head up I had to ask that question sir. It's standard."

"Did my wife wire you the amount of money requested?"

"Yes she did. Don't worry everything is financially taken care of. I thoroughly looked over your file. Your charges are, breaking and entering and two counts of first degree murder. Let me give you some details on how all of this works Mr. Massingil. In a few days you will be arraigned. More than likely the judge will deny your bond considering the atrocity of these charges. Don't get discouraged during this time at all, winning a case like this will take time. I want to apply my truest effort to extricate you from this situation." Passion observed the sad look on Omar's face.

"Hey Omar, I was built for cases like this. After we win you must promise me one thing?"

"What is that Passion?"

"I would love to have your autograph. You're my favorite player. I've been watching you ever since your career started in College. You played for Auburn when you guys won the championship. You were first round draft pick in 2011." Omar smiled from ear to ear. "Yes, I'm a true fan," smiled Passion.

"Well I appreciate your energy and hopefully you can see me through this mess. Hell, I'll sign every article you have if we win!" smiled Omar.

Although the relationship between Terry and his daughter strengthened, his snort habit had progressed to an all-time high and was uncontrollable. His frequent mood swings caused his daughter to become uneasy. Terry noticed her sadness and knew he had to kick his habit. When he was sober he was the perfect father, but when he was high, he was merely a stranger. He vowed that once he kicked his habit, she would never see him like that again. After he took her home he contemplated what had to be done. While in deep thought the phone rung, it was Mariah.

"Hey Terry, what are you and your shorty doing over there?"

"I just took her home Mariah."

"Why so soon? Is everything okay?"

"Well actually it's not sis. You remember when you told me that in order for me to be the father I need to be, I need to kill this habit?"

"Yes I do," replied Mariah.

"Well I'm at my breaking point Sis," Terry had tears in his voice. "I'm allowing this habitual demon to get in the way of the relationship with my daughter. I admit, I really do need some help. Seem like she was ready to go home and could tell my mood had changed. That hurt my soul to the core."

"First of all, you had no business being around her like that Terry. That's crazy as hell."

"I know sis, I do. I damn sure don't want to jeopardize what we've already established. So, what should I do?"

"Well bro listen, I'm on my way. We're about to nip this shit in the bud. Not only do you have to be a father to your daughter, we still have business to handle. Do you know how pissed Passion would be if she found out you be high all the time?"

"Yeah I know. Well how are you going to get here? Didn't you tell me your car was down?"

"I'm on my way man. Matter of fact I'm about to call a jitney."

CHAPTER FIFTEEN

Terry opened the door and observed Mariah carrying two suitcases.

"Look like somebody is about to move in!"

"Until you get better, hell yeah. One thing you're not about to do is mess up my money. On top of that this is for your own good. Do you have a problem with that?" asked Mariah.

"Not at all, but what is your plan?" Terry asked.

"Well we're about to lock ourselves in this house until you drop kick this demon. At times you'll hate me but it's for your own good. Trust me Terry, years ago, someone did the exact same thing for me. You'll thank me later. After my daughter died, I was strung out."

"Whatever happened to your daughter anyway. I mean how did she die?"

"Right now Terry, I would rather not talk about that. Let's focus on you, but I'll explain it all in due time okay."

"I understand Mariah but don't forget, I consider you to be like a sister to me. I appreciate how you have shown me loyalty, which is something I'm not used to in my life. I'm just saying sis! It's only right for me to be an ear to listen sometimes." Terry held his head down.

"Okay bro let's change the channel and focus on you. You got food in them cupboards man?"

"Yeah, it's plenty of food in there so make yourself at home," said Terry.

"Terry I just need to get a few things off my chest. I know how you hate for me to sound like I'm nagging or preaching but we both know my presence here is needed." Terry dropped his chin a few inches. "At the end of the day, we have a job to do that requires sobriety. On top of all that, where can we find a job right now making the kind of money that Passion is about to pay us? We have obligated ourselves to be her assassins and we must finish our end of the bargain. We need that cash bro you feel me, and Candace needs you to survive." Terry and Mariah locked eyes and fist pumped.

"I'm up for this challenge sis. Don't worry. I just hope you can deal with seeing me at my worst," smiled Terry.

****

A few weeks had passed before Terry felt some self-control and Mariah was there every step of the way. She refused to allow him to leave the house and even hid his cell phone. On day twelve he begged her to let him leave and even tried to sneak his way out, but he didn't have enough strength to force his way out of the door.

"Mariah please. I need some bad man. I feel like I'm dying!" Mariah just ignored him as tears fell from her eyes as she witnessed the moment.

"Terry you're not going anywhere and you're not dying you're overcoming. If I let you go your life will be over. Do you not understand that?" yelled Mariah. Terry was faced with a loss of appetite, cold sweats and continuous shakes. One night he shook so bad Mariah was one second away from calling the ER. Instead she held him close like a baby until he finally went to sleep. That was the last night he trembled. They survived it together which made their bond stronger. As days passed he slowly embraced his sobriety challenge.

He would wake up at seven a.m. doing push-ups, sit ups and shadow boxing in place for cardio. On the final day of locking him in the house, Terry woke up and smelled breakfast. Mariah was making chicken wings, cheese eggs, waffles, fried potatoes and a side of pineapple.

"Good Morning sis!" Terry smiled as he hugged her.

"Terry I'm so proud of you. You deserve this breakfast bro. Do you feel like you're ready to begin recovery outside of these walls or what? I mean don't get me wrong, I'm committed to seeing you become sober but, I'm tired of being cooped up." Mariah chuckled.

"Put it like this, right now, this is the strongest I've felt in a long time. I owe you so much sis."

"Well everybody needs somebody. It's all good."

****

Omar Massingil was denied bond and forced to await trial in the county jail. Judge Tassell was assigned to this case and that didn't sit well with Passion. Tassell was a well-known racist, however the eloquence

Passion displayed in the presence of the jurors always played a huge part in her winning cases. Yet and still she felt threatened by judge Tassell and decided it was time to turn to her two assassins for their support. After Terry received the information he needed from Passion, they were on the first flight from Omaha Eppley Airfield to Oakland International. Although they were headed to do what they were hired to do, they were excited to swap twenty-five-degree weather for palm trees and plenty of sunshine.

Disguised in their appearance they motioned for a taxi to take them to the car rental location. Now they were in motion to purchase some firearms. Mariah purchased the guns while Terry waited in the car. She returned with two semi-automatics and a conniving smile.

"Looks like everything went smooth," said Terry.

"Of course," replied Mariah smiling as she took off her dark black shades.

"Let's go get something to eat," said Terry as he slowly pulled away.

Judge Julie Tassell and her husband John were seated in their living room having a political debate. Although they'd been married for close to forty years, they were opposite in many ways. John was months away from retiring and was ready to explore the world. Judge Tassell downplayed his new-found energy and John felt as though his wife had an old folk mentality. He didn't agree with her views on politics and was far from a racist. Seemed as though a great debate was always a conversation away, but contrary to her hateful unethical ways of thinking, they loved one another unconditionally.

"Julie, you are part of this corrupted system so what's the use in debating about it. You're fully aware that I don't agree with the systematic structure here in America. There's too many lives at stake here. Police are killing minorities like they're hunting wild animals for a living. Our prisons are over populated with minorities with non-violent offenses, while white America execute far more heinous acts in this society. Let's not forget to mention the fact that it's covered up by white people with power. It just doesn't sit well with me." John got up and walked towards the dining room to grab a glass of wine.

"John, that was a white lady that nigger ran over. He didn't have a license to drive and that could've been my mother."

"For Christ sakes Julie, your mother Is dead!" yelled John.

"What an ignorant thing to say John!"

"I'm sorry Julie, I just don't want to debate about this right now!"

"Well I'm sorry you always feel the need to disagree with your wife of forty years. It's my job and I'm sorry that I feel the need to talk it out with my husband. You are my husband, right?"

"Can we just have one moment where we can sip our wine, relax and let the courthouse stay downtown?"

"Why are you always in opposition?" questioned Julie while rolling her eyes and sipping her wine.

"Julie let's not go there.........the sound of the doorbell invaded their debate. John sat his glass down and got up to answer the door. "Who could this be at this time of the night." He squinted one eye through the peephole of the door. It was a negro woman appearing to be old in age. "How may I help you?" asked John. He couldn't clearly hear her, so he unchained and opened the door. Julie was looking over his shoulder.

"Sorry about this inconvenience, but my car broke down about a half mile up the road and I have no service on my cell phone sir. Would you mind allowing me to use your phone to call my son for some help? That would be such a blessing," said Mariah sporting an old-fashioned wig with bifocals on.

"Hold on for a second ma'am," replied John as he closed the door to converse with Julie.

"Why did she come here for help?" Julie asked skeptically.

"Honey you know these houses are secluded and cell phones don't work in this area. Just let me handle this

122

okay." Julie went back into the living room and sat down. John grabbed the cordless phone and walked outside on the porch. Julie didn't agree with helping a black woman let alone allowing her to use their phone, but she didn't want to interfere with what seemed like a harmless situation. He handed her the phone.

"Thanks sir," smiled Mariah revealing a nice set of white teeth. Mariah could tell he was scrutinizing her.

Suddenly her disguised look became apparent to John. Noticing her skin was smooth, he also observed that her teeth and eyes displayed a youthful glow. It became apparent that her wig, glasses, and attire she was wearing was a facade. John instantly became nervous.

"Ma'am you can take your time using the phone. Just ring the doorbell when you're finished."

As John started walking towards the front door, in a split second he felt the barrel of a gun pressed against the back of his head.

"Scream, yell, or do anything to arouse your wife, and I will blow your motherfucking head off without hesitation."

"What do you want from us? How could we possibly be of any interest to you?" John whispered as his voice trembled.

"I really want to talk to your wife so let's walk inside. I won't hurt either of you as long as you both cooperate."

"We will ma'am," replied John. Julie's eyes were lit up as they walked slowly into the house. It didn't take long for her to realize that there was something terribly wrong. She stood up abruptly.

"John! What is going on?" Mariah shoved him over to his wife.

"Shut the hell up you old rag doll! I've heard so many stories about your old prejudice ass. You don't like black people huh? ANSWER ME!" yelled Mariah as she pointed the gun in her face.

"Please don't hurt my wife. She's a good woman. Take me instead."

"She's far from good she's a racist bitch," said Mariah.

"Listen honey, we're all children of God. She may have some flaws, as we all do, but deep down inside there's a good heart. Please don't hurt my wife." John tried to pull her heartstrings praying she would listen. Mariah looked in Julie's fearful eyes.

"Judge Tassell! How many lives have you railroaded? How many harsh sentences have you handed down to black people who didn't deserve it?"

"I'm so sorry.........please don't hurt us!" Julie begged as she cried hoping Mariah would spare her life.

"Judge Tassell! You have sat your stanky ass on that bench for years separating black families and turning your nose up at minorities. Who in the fuck do you think you are? Is it a coincidence that most white collar criminals who stand before you receive probation, or little to no jail time? Not only have your actions been heartless, but despicable. Not to mention, I just stood outside your window and listened to the entire conversation you and your husband had, and I

124

thought to myself. 'This is the way this bitch really feels!' I mean I was in total shock to hear that shit and that was very disturbing. The sad part is that your husband's life is about to end because he married a low down dirty racist bitch like you. Today, I'm the judge and I'm sending your ass straight to hell bitch." Before they begged any further, John and Julie were slaughtered by Mariah's wrath.

CHAPTER SIXTEEN

With Judge Tassell being murdered, Omar Massingil was granted an honest judge which in return he received a fair trial. Both victims were brutally stabbed to death in their home, and Omar's skin was left in his ex-wife fingernails. The prosecutor argued that a struggle took place between them which led to her death. Omar's testimony conveyed that they made love a few hours before the double homicide occurred. He also stated that his ex-wife mentioned the fear of a guy that she'd been courting for only a few weeks. Allegedly he was extremely angry that she'd broke things off.

After an exhausting two-week trial, Passion was able to prove reasonable doubt and miraculously, Omar Massingil was found not guilty.

"Passion you're truly an angel and I cannot thank you enough," smiled Omar.

"Well you can start off by signing this picture for your biggest fan." Passion stayed in California to soak up a few more days of sunshine before returning home.

She returned to work with several caseloads ahead of her. Before she retired her first day of being back on the job, Bill called and stated that a prior male client was waiting in the front lobby to see her.

"Send him in," replied Passion. As her office door slowly opened she realized it was once again Shawn.

"Why are you here Shawn?" He shut and locked her office door behind him.

"I just wanted to make myself clear."

"Clear about what?"

"Well I didn't express myself with clarity," said Shawn.

"What clarity? What in the world are you talking about?" asked Passion as she took off her glasses and stood up. "You raped me and now you're stalking me. I don't deal with the police for free, but do I need a restraining order on you or what?" Shawn eyes roamed over her beautiful figure noticing her tight pencil skirt, fitted white button up, and sexy black red bottom heels. "Hello....hello...... um SHAWN," yelled Passion "So you really want to try me I see," she threatened.

"No baby. I want you to try me! I promise it will be better than the last time," whispered Shawn as he grinned slyly. Passion was shocked by his audacity and couldn't believe that he was walking around the desk to get closer. Her resistance melted in his arms as she gave in to his kiss.

Suddenly the kiss turned passionate after she realized that her body has been craving for this moment. In one sudden motion Shawn swept everything off Passions desk and she was eager to oblige the moment. As she laid down on the desk, Shawn began to caress her breast while she unbuckled his belt at the same time. She roughly pulled off his shirt while he lifted her skirt and they began to create a magic that was unbelievable. Passion had no control over the moment as Shawn stroked inside of her with force. Attempting to silence some of her screams, Shawn put his fingers in her mouth, but it didn't work.

Ron and Charlena were at the courthouse which made the office unusually quiet, however Bill, her secretary could not believe what he was hearing. His ears were ringing as he sat close to her office door ejaculating to the sounds of Passions moans. Shawn turned her over and began penetrating her from the back. With her elbows on the desk, she could hardly handle him as he jabbed himself inside her aggressively. An orgasm washed over her so intense that her whole body felt as though it had locked up. Begging him to stop only made them both thrust back harder at one another.

"Don't cum inside me!" He obeyed her command as he pulled out quickly and sprayed his semen on her lower back. As they both sat still momentarily, Passion appeared frustrated.

"Get that stuff off of me and get out!" Shawn obeyed. She gave him his shirt and told him to never come back again. Shawn pulled her in for another deep kiss and once again she met his passion. After five more intense minutes of kissing, they broke away. Shawn dressed himself quickly. Slowly walking to her door with a huge grin on his face, he placed his phone number on the table.

"Use it baby. Whenever you need me again I'll come running."

Passion sat there exhausted and confused.

"Damn! Once again I allowed the moment to defeat me, but damn that was some good ass lovin." Passion shook her head and smiled.

****

Although Passion had plenty of fans celebrating with her, she also had a few who hated the ground she walked on. One onlooker sat at home watching her speak about the Omar Massingil trial and was wishing death upon her.

"A champion at freeing criminals huh. That little pretty bitch got hers coming." When she observed the 'Not Guilty' verdict she turned off her television unable to bare the sight of her smiling in victory.

After a few months of being separated from Passion, Tiara had finally realized that their friendship had ran its course. A relationship that she once believed was infrangible had come to an end. A tremendous amount of grief weighed upon her and Shawn was her solace. Although she loved him deeply, inside her soul she felt like something was missing. Shawn didn't possess the attraction nor the mental stimulation that Passion did.

She missed how appreciative Passion was when she did things that made her day and listening to the joyous sounds of her laughter. Her inner beauty as well as physical attributes overshadowed anyone she'd ever met, but Tiara had to soak it in.

After a few months of not even a word from Passion, Tiara finally started to move on. Until one-night Shawn came home smelling like a familiar fragrance. When Tiara disengaged from his embrace she was in shock and disbelief. Shawn noticed it and instantly realized his mistake.

"What's wrong bae?" asked Shawn.

"You just gone play me like I'm a damn x-box huh?"

"What in the hell are you talking about lady?" questioned Shawn.

"You know what I smell and who I smell."

"Girl you're on some bullshit right now! What do you mean who you smell?" He frowned and put his nose to his collar and sniffed.

"Yeah, that's Passion you dirty son of a bitch. So, yaw stayed at it huh? Wow!"

"See Tiara this is why we stay at odds because you always assume and make a complete ass out of yourself. Yes! I did go to Passion's office. Damn you know I had to pay off the balance from my case. I took her the twenty-five hundred I owed her, we hugged, she said take care, and that was it!" Tiara folded her arms up to her chest.

"Did you fuck her? Falling up in this bitch smelling like Ellie Saab and shit. Nobody from this neighborhood even knows about that fragrance other than Passion." Tiara smelled his neck once again. Shawn pushed her away from him.

"Tiara look! STOP ACCUSING ME OF BULLSHH.".........
Shawn stopped abruptly and took a deep breath as he observed her wipe a tear from the corner of her eye.

"See here we go with this shit. Now you're about to cry. Tiara listen, you're crying for no damn reason. I seriously don't wanna hear nothing else you have to say. Crying like you're at a got damn funeral. You done lost your mind, but guess what Tiara? If you continue on with this nonsense you gone lose me." Shawn quickly grabbed his towel and headed towards the bathroom to shower and slammed the door.

Tiara began to cry as reality set in. Life felt like it was dilapidated, and it seemed as though she had no one to turn to. For the first time in her life, she felt completely alone.

After that sexual encounter at the office Passion was eager to fit Shawn into her schedule. She purchased a bungalow outside of the city. A rustic area surrounded by endless woods, deer trails, waterfalls, and a huge lake for fishing made the setting beautiful. Swallowed in privacy she loved the serene scenery and thought it was a great sanatorium to hide away from the world. Passion was pleased with the hardwood floors, exquisite furniture and enormous fireplace. Not only was it spacious, the view from the bedroom window was breathtaking.

Shawn saw this new place for the first time and instantly fell in love with the setup. He couldn't believe that for the first time in his life, he was actually being upgraded. He had a few dollars, but his money was nowhere near long enough to provide this type of experience for a woman. After an evening full of laughs, a romantic dinner, and a bubble bath in the Jacuzzi, they made love all night long.

There was something about Passion that made Shawn fall deep in love. Recognizing that beauty and sex shouldn't be the main reason to fall in love, the fact that Passion saved his life was a momentary suffice. After an intense round of love making, Passion let out a chuckle to break up the silence.

"What's funny boo?" asked Shawn. Passion hated to be called boo but overlooked that and gave him an honest reply.

"Well, just how crazy life is. I mean I'm addicted to you which is something I'd never thought would happen," smiled Passion. He rolled over and snuggled into her astounded by her revelation.

"What If I told you I was in love with you?" asked Shawn.

"Well, that's something I prefer not to hear," she replied with her eyes glued to the ceiling.

"What, you don't think you can love a person who was accused of murdering someone. If that's the reason, then why are you fucking me every night Passion?" Shawn sat up in the bed waiting for a reply. Passion sat up as well.

"First of all, Shawn, calm down. Secondly, I'm a criminal lawyer and in order for me to be the best I must remain conscientious towards my clients. Besides, we all have skeletons. Passion pulled in close to Shawn and softly kissed him on the lips. "Let's just enjoy the moment." Shawn heart started beating after the kiss.

"Passion girl, you know you got me wide open! Don't you?"

CHAPTER SEVENTEEN

Passion Veland was now labeled one of the top three lawyers of America. Young, rich, and invincible, and with the help of her assassins, she hadn't lost another case. Now running with employees who were superb at their job, Veland's Law Firm became the biggest law firm in the country. Terry and Mariah were paid well and treated their job like they were drafted by the military swat team. Tolerating long hours of work by studying targets and planning out their attacks with precision, and they meant business.

Passion admired their work ethic and was pleased with how business was flowing. Even though she wanted to spend more time with Mariah and Terry she knew it was best for them to meet at selected hotels, however when they agglomerate it wasn't only about business. They laughed, talked, and caught themselves up to speed on past encounters. Passion also warned them about reckless purchases. Any items purchased over nine thousand had to be approved through her to avoid the I.R.S. tapping in.

Passion and Shawn still had a liaison, but it was shallow. She never allowed their sexual encounters to blossom into anything other than, a sexual encounter. Not only was he well hung and professional with his tongue, his stamina was mind blowing to say the least. He wasn't a ten-stroke kind of guy, but she made it clear that outside of their liaison in bed, she didn't have any feelings for him whatsoever.

Thanks to Tiara's episode, Passion's desire for men was at an all-time high. As time went on Passion met a guy who she became very fond of and started dating which eliminated Shawn from the picture.

Pierre Black, a thirty-year old bank executive with a name that matched his complexion. Dark skinned, six feet one, perfect teeth, and built like an Olympic sprinter. She wasn't too impressed with him sexually however his personality outweighed everything. His divorce was finalized nine months ago, and meeting Passion was a breath of fresh air. For the next few months they spent all their weekends together.

****

Passion and Tiara never reconciled. Word had gotten back to Passion that Shawn and Tiara had broken things off once she found out he was still sleeping with her. Tiara's life had turned into a whirlwind. She started boosting out of shopping malls but was far from a good thief. Caught a few misdemeanors and found herself at rock bottom. Coming from the lavish lifestyle she once lived, she believed that hustling was the only way to have nice things again. Tiara met a guy name Deandre Tucker from Cleveland, Ohio and moved down the way. She didn't realize that 40th and Quincy was a city all by itself. You had to be tough to survive in that area. Deandre convinced her that he had plenty of money stashed away, but once they arrived, Tiara became the money maker. Prostitution, drug dealing, and check scamming were her means of income and soon the Feds rained on her parade. Tiara was arrested and charged with solicitation, forgery, and unauthorized use of a financial transaction. Too ashamed to call Passion, she received a sentence of two to five years in the Northeast Ohio Correctional Institution. For a while Passion didn't know what was going on in Tiara's life. Occasionally she would call Shawn and ask of her whereabouts, but he had lost contact with her as well. Passion finally got in touch with Tiara's mother who told her everything.

Although their relationship faded, she still loved Tiara and never wanted to see her in that type of predicament.

Passion immediately went to the post office and sent Tiara a short heartfelt postcard.

Dear Tiara,

I just spoke with Mama T. She told me where I could find you. Well needless to say I didn't expect her to say this place. Although we have remained distant, I still love you and want what's best for you. When my granny died, you were the 'ANGEL' I needed in my life and I will always love you for being there for me during one of the worst stages in my life. She also told me you don't have much longer to go in that place so if you need anything don't hesitate to call me okay.

(402) 453-5756 Sincerely, Passion.

Passion felt rueful to a certain degree. Although Tiara's deceptive act destroyed their close relationship, revenge didn't exist in Passion's heart. Ever since the threesome occurred, Passion never desired another woman. Thanks to Tiara that stage of her life was over, nevertheless she deeply missed her friendship.

Passion had just finished cooking a country breakfast for Pierre.

"Smells like the beginning of a beautiful day in here, but staring at a beautiful woman is even better," said Pierre as he wrapped his arms around her from behind.

"Thank you baby. This is all for a beautiful man." Her lips reached for his as they kissed. "Now that was refreshing! You got the newspaper baby?" asked Passion?"

"You know I do."

They would often eat and browse through the newspaper to keep up on current events. Although they both had smartphones, they wanted to stay away from social media to avoid laughing at all the foolery. Pierre felt there was a time and place for social media and took his morning reads with Passion very serious.

She browsed through the housing foreclosure section. Over the years she had invested in several rental properties and doubled her savings account. However today, she had Tiara in mind. Passion wanted to find something very affordable for her to come home to. Saddened about the lifestyle Tiara chose, she was eager to help get her life back on track.

"Such a beautiful view," said Pierre as he gazed through the kitchen window. Passion looked up from the paper and roamed her eyes over nature's irrefutable beauty. The sun was standing high over the clear blue endless lake, while a hawk soared through the rays of the scintillating sun.

Deer gathered along the trail lapping water fully aware that it was hunting season. This bungalow was Passion's peace, solace and most cherished property.

Later that day they decided to have a barbecue cookout by the lake. Passion invited employees from the firm and Pierre invited some buddies over. While the guys stood around talking sports, and drinking beer, the women kicked back and enjoyed the moments of jocularity. Passion could tell the barbecue grill was something Pierre mastered. While admiring his work Terry and Mariah came to mind.

"I've got to see those two fools today," she mumbled while grabbing her cell phone. "Hey honey I'm going to step away for a second and call my cousins I haven't seen them in forever."

"Ok beautiful. I can't wait to meet them," said Pierre as he kissed her softly on the lips.

"Hello, Hi Terry," said Passion.

"Who dis?"

"It's me Passion!"

"Hey! What's up babe?"....... (he caught himself). "I mean, nothing just chillin with my daughter watching a movie. What you up to miss lady?"

"Not much really. Have you spoke with Mariah lately?"

"Nah, well not today. Is there another assignment due?"

"That's not why I'm calling. I'm having a small gathering. Basically, a welcoming barbecue cookout at my place near Cunningham Lake. There's a few nice people out here and it's totally safe. I miss you guys and thought this would be a great opportunity to meet Evelyn." Terry was surprised by the invitation and didn't want to make a detrimental mistake. She read into his thoughts. "Don't worry everything is copacetic. Just a few friends from the firm, my guy friend and a few of his buddies."

"Well as long as you say it's cool then I'll get a hold a Mariah and we'll be on our way."

"Hey Terry?"

"What's up!"

"Remember, you guys are my cousins okay?"

"I got you!" Terry was tickled.

After she gave him directions, she grabbed a bud light out of the cooler and headed back towards the cookout. Around six thirty a silver Ford Escape pulled up and Passion noticed it was Terry, Evelyn and Mariah.

Passion embraced them all and hugged Evelyn whom seemed a bit shy.

"My goodness Terry she's a spitting image of you. You must be Evelyn. My name is Passion. I've heard so many good things about you and oh my goodness you're beautiful and I love your hair."

"Thank you!" replied Evelyn.

"Wow Terry her mother sure does do a great job taking care of her hair!" Terry and Mariah were smiling as they admired her land.

"Girl now this right here, is definitely living," said Mariah.

"You like it girl?" smiled Passion.

"Like it? I love it!" said Mariah with a serious look on her face. Passion introduced them to her company and everyone socialized in harmony which turned out to be a zestful evening.

Passion watched Terry and Mariah as they walked down close to the water and sat adjacently on a bench. Passion was unaware of the dark secrets kept between them but assumed they'd endured some trials. Reminiscing back when she first met Terry at the sports bar with her business proposal. She remembered him mentioning something about his baby mother was using his daughter against him. When she asked him to elaborate, he killed the subject. Within that time, she knew he had closed the gap and the look in his eyes revealed so much.

Respecting his diligence of becoming a father and his natural swag is why Passion was always attracted to him. He had a sexy way about himself that she found to be magnetic and it resonated through his voice, his eyes, the way he moved and his glow. Passion ignored this feeling for a long time considering business was the primary liaison, but it couldn't be ignored any longer.

CHAPTER EIGHTEEN

Everyone was seated outside relaxing on the patio furniture sipping Patron Tequilas listening to Pandora radio. All of the other guest was gone accept Pierre, Mariah, Terry and Evelyn. Observing that the sun was on its way to set, Pierre felt it was the perfect setting to place his arms around Passion.

"Did I do a good job on the grill today baby?" asked Pierre.

"Actually honey, it was like food porn. I didn't know you were a chef kind of guy."

"Well I wouldn't give myself that title, but I know in time my cooking will have you spoiled." Pierre rubbed his mustache in a boastful fashion.

"Well, I think it's a little too late for that. You have me rotten already," smiled Passion.

"Is that right?" Pierre grinned back as they leaned into one another for a soft kiss.

"Passion, I better get Evelyn home so she can get ready for school tomorrow," said Terry.

"Oh no you guys are about to leave? Well hold on let me walk you guys to the car." Passion pecked Pierre on the lips. "I'll be right back honey."

As they slowly walked towards the car Terry put his arms around Passion.

"You know we wanted to get you alone to have a little one on one without him right? I mean no offense towards that guy he seems like a good dude, but you know we can't discuss our business in front of him."

"I totally understand and trust me he knows nothing about nothing. Hell, he barely knows me," laughed Passion.

"Well I know one damn thing girl, he is fine as hell," said Mariah. Passion and Mariah fist pumped.

"Girl yes, he is handsome and smart. I mean he's a good guy but I'm finding it hard to get into him. I know that's weird huh? Can I tell you guys something since I consider you guys like family? Wait...hey Terry you should let Evelyn go swing for 15 minutes."

"Oh ok. Ev baby we're about to discuss some business. Do you wanna swing for a little while?"

"Yayyyyy! Thanks dad. I wasn't ready to leave yet."

"Alright sweetie." Evelyn skipped to the swings.

"Okay here's the deal and don't laugh. Are you guys ready for this?"

"Girl just spit it out," said Mariah.

"I HATE HAVING SEX WITH HIM." Mariah and Terry busted out laughing. "Yeah I knew you guys would laugh." Terry laughed the hardest. "Okay Mr. Tickled pink. Why are you laughing so hard?"

"Passion, I'm sorry, I just didn't expect that to come out of your mouth that's all. It's all good girl don't trip. It just threw me off guard," Terry said as he started coughing from laughing so hard.

"Well I'm glad you're getting a kick out of it silly man." Mariah chuckled while watching them laugh.

"Well Passion I'll have to agree with you on that one honey. Sex is a huge factor. What about his oral game?" asked Mariah.

"Aw shit now hold on ladies. Do I really have to listen to the way that man handles his business?" asked Terry.

"He does not eat the vagina," laughed Passion.

"Aw hell naw. I need you to tell him where to go boss lady. Life is too short for that bullshit. Matter of fact he aint' even cute no more. Boy bye!" said Mariah as she rolled her eyes.

"Girl I'm about to lose my mind because I'm sexually frustrated," Passion said quietly.

"Okay let me change the channel ladies. I'm thinking about copping me a V-Twelve Kawasaki. They want fifteen stacks for it, so I may need your assistance Passion if that's okay? asked Terry.

"Well first of all, do you understand how dangerous those bikes are?" asked Passion.

"Girl I've told him that more than once," cosigned Mariah. Terry laughed.

"It sure does feel good to see two of my favorite ladies expressing concern for ya boy!"

"Well just let me know when you want to make that happen but promise me you'll be careful on it? said Passion.

Shawn was obliviously stalked for some time now and tonight the stalker had plans to end his life. He stopped at a hole in the wall pub to drown his liver with alcohol, frustrated because his life had changed from bad to worse.

"I'll take another double shot of Jack and coke please!" Shawn was on his fifth double shot and was tipping the bartender recklessly. Depression had set in as his days were spent ruminating over the loss of Tiara and Passion's companionship. The thought of Passion made his blood boil. She ignored his text messages and phone calls and that turned his anger into hatred. He often contemplated killing her. Not to mention the Feds came in and swept the entire city, so finding drugs was like looking for a needle in a haystack. Then to top it all off, he missed the sound of Tiara's voice.

He felt she was the only woman who loved him for him. His betrayal alone hurt him deeply because he left her for a woman who had no intentions on loving him.

"High saddity ass triflen bitch. I hate that bitch with a passion. A FUCKING PASSION," he yelled and observed the bartender motion no more drinks for tonight.

"Hey Tom, I'm twisted man!" Shawn slurred and staggered while standing up to leave. Heading out to his vehicle stumbling, Shawn observed Shantae Miles sitting at a table all alone. His heart started beating as he tried to avoid her spotting him. Shantae stood up.

"Hey Shawn." Shawn kept walking as Shantae ran outside behind him.

"Look lady, I don't have time to be in any kind of shit okay. I'm drunk and my life is fucked up. If you wanna see me dead, guess what? This is what the hell death looks like. So, leave me the fuck alone."

"No Shawn, I'm not here to hurt or harm you. I've been praying about all of what happened. You see I'm alone right? Look, I just wanted to talk with you that's all," said Shantae with a sad look on her face.

"Talk about what?" Terry said looking frustrated.

"Well I'll give you my number and we can talk about it later. I'm sure you could use a little money, right?"

Did you say money?" said Shawn as he sobered up a few notches."

"Yes I did! You can call me from a private number, but I really need to talk to you. Since time has passed, I have reason to believe that you're actually innocent. So please call me."

"Damn Shantae that's cool. Hell yeah I'll call you." Shawn hopped in his vehicle and smiled.

"Damn she's beautiful. Shakeem was one stupid son of a bitch because that baby mama Malaysia looked like Sho-nuff from the Last Dragon. His stupid ass didn't belong on this earth leaving something like that behind no way." Shawn giggled and talked to himself the entire ride home listening to Tupac's Me against the world c.d.

****

Passion and Tiara were reunited in friendship for the remainder of Tiara's jail term and with just sixty days left of her sentence she was mentally prepared to embrace and face any challenges ahead. Tiara respected the fact that Passion was no longer a lesbian, but thoughts of changing that stayed in the back of her mind. Tiara prayed that Passion would change her mind once she was in her presence again.

Passion wanted Tiara to come home to a fresh start. She loved her and had the means to provide some simple luxuries, so she made it happen. A home, car, clothes, and a secretarial job at the firm awaited her in Omaha.

Day by day throughout her incarceration, she yearned for Passion's touch. Missing her beautiful smile and the unique sound of her laugh. Ever since their separation her cravings grew stronger and she was anxious to recapture what she thought was forever lost. Although jail had plenty of women who dreamed of playing house while in prison with her, she couldn't see herself with any other women, and after Shawn and Deandre.......men were totally out of the question.

TIARA'S RELEASE DAY!

"My goodness! Tiara! Jail really does preserve. You look amazing," said Passion with tears in her eyes.

"Thank you. Passy you look beautiful too. Time has definitely been on your side boo," smiled Tiara.

"I want you to meet my man. His name is Pierre." Pierre stepped in closer.

"Wow she's beautiful just like you said honey! What a pleasure to finally meet my baby's best friend!" Tiara accepted his hug as she gazed at Passion appearing happy that the two of them finally met. Passion made breakfast served with wine and they all talked in harmony.

"Baby, I know you guys have plenty to catch up on so I'm going to the office. I have some work to finish. It's been hectic lately," said Pierre as he leaned in for a kiss. "It was nice to finally meet you Tiara."

"Likewise," said Tiara.

After Pierre left, an awkward silence filled the room as they briefly stared at one another.

"Do you love him?" Passion sighed as if she knew this was coming. Is he the reason we can't rebuild what we once had?" asked Tiara.

"First of all Tee, I care for Pierre but not how you think. When it comes to us, what we had more than anything was a genuine friendship. You were and still is my sister regardless of how sexual things used to be. You've always been there for me throughout the good and bad, but back then I didn't have a grip on my sexuality. Well now I know what I want and that's a man, but I'm your friend until the end." Tiara's eyes began to fill with tears.

"Well I guess that answered all of my questions and killed my hopes all at the same damn time. Maybe in time you'll have a change of heart and come back to me the way I need you too. I appreciated your support Pas and.".......... Passion cut her off.

"Tiara, there's no need to thank me. If I got it, you got it, and please don't cry okay. I need for you to understand this situation without letting my decisions hurt you." Tiara wiped the tears from her eyes.

"I guess I don't have a choice Pas." They hugged one another tightly and headed out the door to go visit family. After spending the rest of the day together, Passion dropped her off and headed home. She prepared for her nightly routine which consisted of taking a bubble bath, listening to Jazz, and sipping on a glass of wine to wind down for the night. A green light notification was on her cell phone. Passion opened an incoming text message from Pierre.

"Hey baby, you want some of King Cobra tonight? I miss you boo. We haven't talked all day. Just call me Passion and I'll come running. Love you."

Passion frowned up her nose at the language of the text.

"Ugh he erks my nerves Lord. This man is boring as hell and sounds like he is seventy-two years old talking about some damn king cobra. Shit you mean more like a damn garter snake ugh." Passion mumbled while laughing at the same time. She never loved Shawn but missed the way he felt inside of her and the more wine she sipped, the more she desired some lovin from a man other than Pierre. Shawn was out of the question because she knew he was a stalker, but the last glass of wine gave her enough courage to call Terry.

"Hey Terry. This is Passion."

"Hey boss! What's up with you," said Terry.

"Well I was wondering if you would come over. I really need an ear to listen tonight. Also"......(Passion Paused)

"Hello!" Are you there?" Terry questioned in a confused like tone.

"I may need you to give me a little something. Never mind just come over."

"Something like what? Have you been drinking boss?"

"First of all, I'm your boss when it's time to be your boss and nothing will sidetrack that but as of right now, I'm not your boss."

"You're not expecting anyone are you?" Terry questioned.

"This is my house don't worry about all that."

"Hmm, Okay Passion I'll be over there to chop it up with you. You know it's gone take me about forty-five minutes to get there right?"

"Yep and I'll be waiting."

CHAPTER NINETEEN

After the first sexual encounter they instantly became addicted to one another. The no fraternization rule was broken but they agreed to remain discreet.

Pierre observed a difference in her behavior and realized her walk was different. She had an extra step in her strut with a zestful vibe that he'd never noticed before. Although he didn't question her about her exuberance, she was definitely under his scrutiny.

As time passed, their feelings for one another turned into love. A feeling Passion had never experienced with a man before. Her relationship with Pierre faded, not to mention Terry was tired of sharing her. She was ready to cut her ties with Pierre and become sacred with Terry. For that to happen, she knew a change would have to happen as well.

"Where are you?" Passion asked.

"I just dropped Evelyn off at her mother's house."

"You're in traffic?"

"Yep, is everything okay?" questioned Terry.

"Well we really need to talk. Can you come by my office when you have a chance?"

"I'm on my way right now."

Ever since Passion and Terry had become involved, the assassin job was put on the back burner.

The Veland Law Firm reputation had an eloquent effect on the courts and Passion realized she no longer needed assassins to win cases. Anyone who was in opposition felt inferior and it showed dramatically. Passion received a call from Bill informing her of Terry's arrival.

"Send him back Bill and no interruptions until my meeting is over with. Thanks."

"Yes ma'am." After Bill sent him back, he grabbed his Bluetooth and pressed a button that connected to a wireless microphone wiretap device he had placed underneath Passion's desk. Considering his major in college was computer technology and his hobby was fixing computers, he discreetly bugged her office while everyone was out on duty. Whenever male clients went into her office, he would eavesdrop hoping to catch her in another sexual drive by. To label him obsessed' was an understatement.

"Hey honey!" Passion stepped out from behind her desk and embraced him with a hug and a kiss. "Did you and Ev have a nice weekend together?"

"We had a ball. We went to the movies, played board games, you know, the whole nine yards. Yeah it was nice. I love seeing my baby happy. Oh yeah, we went to an all you can eat buffet. You can definitely tell that she's my daughter man. She ate everything."

"Aww I wish I could've been with you guys."

"She wanted you to come too baby. All she kept saying was daddy where is Passion. I told her you were busy though, she understood," smiled Terry.

"I've been putting off a lot of my work here lately. You know I have that serious trial next week that I plan on winning. Make sure you tell my girl that I'll be there the next time," smiled Passion. "Is she showing progress in math?"

"Funny you asked. I helped her with her math homework last night, and I was stuck. I said hell, maybe I need to go back to school. Math was not my favorite subject, but her teacher said she's acing all of her quizzes. So, you called, and I came running. What's going on miss lady. Talk to me."

"Well I've been thinking about how close we've grown and the joy I receive when I'm spending time with you and Evelyn. I just think it's about time for us to discuss where we're going from here. I don't know about you but I'm ready to take this relationship to another level." Passion stared at Terry in his eyes.

"What about Pierre? Are you ready to totally cut him off because if we decide to make this happen these discreet days are over! You feel me?"

"Yes, I feel you one hundred percent. Pierre who?" They both chuckled and pecked each other on the lips. "So, the reason I rushed you over here is because with us moving forward, I'm omitting the assassin jobs. I'm in love with you Terry and I don't want you to risk your life or what we share by killing or getting killed. I have accomplished so many goals in my life, but never have I experienced what true love and having a family

151

is all about. I've definitely found that love with you guys."

"Awww Passion give me a kiss baby. I have no objections and I love you too. Man, it's just crazy because I never saw this coming and I love the you in you. With your fine self. Damn Passion you're so beautiful. Not only on the outside, but on the inside as well and I feel like the luckiest man alive believe that," smiled Terry.

"Aww babe thank you and ditto," replied Passion.

"Okay so how do I tell Mariah about all this. I mean she takes this job serious and you know she's like my sister," said Terry.

"Well I'm one step ahead of you on that. I have the perfect position for her at the firm. We can both sit her down and talk with her in person about it all."

"That's what's up boo! You must be ready to get married. We may as well hit up the courthouse asap," smiled Terry.

"Hold on wait a minute now! You're moving a little bit too fast for me!"

"Hey I tried," smiled Terry.

CHAPTER TWENTY

Bill leaned back in his chair flabbergasted over what he'd just heard. Although it was discovered from the horse's mouth, he couldn't fathom that something like this happened. Bill snatched the ear bulbs out and sat down slowly trying to gather himself. He felt like if they were to catch him spying, he would become the next target. He noticed Passion and Terry walking towards his desk. Shakily he shuffled through some paperwork with his heartbeat in overdrive trying to appear busy.

"Bill why are you so red? Are you ok?" asked Passion as she slowly walked towards the exit.

"Yes, I'm fine. I just feel myself coming down with a cold, that's all, but thanks for asking."

She walked Terry to his car.

"What's on your agenda this evening?" asked Terry as he observed Passion staring at some bushes next to her office window. "What's the matter is something wrong?" asked Terry.

"Oh, it's just, I could've swore I saw those bushes move and it's not even windy out here. I don't know. Maybe it's these long work hours making my mind bad."
They both giggled.

"Well we definitely need some relaxation time tonight. How about your new husband cook you some dinner? Does that sound like a plan?"

"Husband huh! That was super cute. Sounds like heaven honey."

"Okay I'll see you around seven then?" smiled Terry.

"Yes, I'll be there. Love you boo!"

"Love you too beautiful."

Passion walked back to her office without giving Bill a single glance. Bill sat in his chair still in shock, and suddenly became paranoid as thoughts of her discovering the wiretap he planted in her office crossed his mind. Passion walked out towards his desk.

"Hey Bill, I see you're working hard filing all these old papers and that is greatly appreciated however I'm exhausted so I'm going home early. Make sure you lock up when you're finished, and I'll see you in the morning."

"Ok I will."

His fear slowly transformed into an exciting desire to investigate all of Passions prior cases. He recalled a case where the judge was changed because of unbeknownst reasons. As his presumptions boiled over he curiously went through the file cabinet and removed over a dozen high profile case folders. Anxiety ran through his veins hoping Passion didn't come back and catch him making copies. That night sleep was hard to find as he laid next to his wife Jennifer who was softly snoring. After pouring a cup of coffee, he shuffled through the files and found out his presumptions were now very true. In every file there was someone connected to that particular case who was murdered right before the trial. Also, each victim was favored by the prosecutor. After a while his memory started to resurface.

There were several witnesses, two Judges, prosecutors,' and even a few cops, who were potential victims. The thought of this whole ordeal made him nervous as he pulled out a pack of Marlboro reds from his duffle bag.

"How many people have you killed Ms. Passion Veland?"

He silently muttered as he dug deeper into contemplation mode realizing he had Passion tangled up in a web that could be detrimental to her career and livelihood.

He juggled three options in his mind. First option was to turn the evidence over to authorities. Second option was to extort her for a large sum of money before turning her into authorities. Third Option. Bribe her for pleasure and money as long as he could before he turned her into the authorities. Although the third option intrigued him, he knew he'd be playing with extreme danger if he decided to take that route. As five a.m. approached he decided to use the excuse of being sick to call into work.

One week passed and his desire to become a puppet master overwhelmed him so he began formulating his approach. The day before he approached Passion, Jennifer questioned him about his whimsical behavior she's been noticing lately. While they were having dinner, he didn't notice he was being scrutinized. Jennifer had always told him that the one thing she would never tolerate in their marriage is a lie.

Bill was always comfortable telling her about his presumptions and felt confident that Jennifer would never share his thoughts with anyone else. She was the only person he trusted with his life. They'd been married for twelve years, together for sixteen and unable to bare children due to the cervical cancer she battled in her early twenties. Although his desire for children was shallow he remained cognizant that one day he would have to become a father to make his wife happy. He sat the fork down and cleared his throat.

"How long have I seemed strange to you honey and what am I doing to make you say that?"

"Lately it's been aloofness with you. Just an awkward silence. Your personality normally shines bright but here lately it's shallow. So, is there something I need to know?"

"Well listen honey, if I tell you what's on my mind you will have to protect the secrecy of this information."

"That's fine, but when did we start questioning the secrecy of what we discuss? See, I told you something was fishy," said Jennifer as she turned beet red wearing an angry smirk stern enough to scare a pit bull.

"Jenn I've always trusted you and you know that. What I mean is, I don't want you gossiping with your nosy sister and brother because this is extremely lethal information." She became rigid.

"Lethal as in dangerous?"

"Extremely dangerous!" She relaxed a bit, so he would feel comfortable explaining his thoughts.

"Okay I'm ready," said Jennifer.

"I think my boss is a killer and have killed many people." Before he went any further he allowed his words to marinate for a few seconds.

"What do you mean your boss is a killer and what makes you assume something like that?" Jennifer was rigid again and began to sweat bullets. Bill didn't reveal the whole truth about how he obtained this information. He explained that he was eavesdropping behind a closed door on the conversation Passion had with one of her hired assassins.

"Maybe she's playing a nasty trick on you and knew you were being nosy. Have you given that some thought Mr. detective?"

"Actually, I have Mrs. Picalo and that is far from the truth. After hearing the conversation, I pulled some of her high-profile case files and guess what?" asked Bill.

"I'm listening!"

"In each and every one of those files somebody was murdered in cold blood. Every cadaver was in opposition of her. Witnesses, judges, a few cops and even a prosecutor. I'm sure there's more. Now I haven't looked through every file because that would literally take all year, but I saw enough to know that nothing I overheard was a game." Jennifer appeared fearful.

"So, if it's true, what do you plan on doing with all of this information? This sounds dangerous and you know my brother has been a cop for twenty years why don't you just".........

Bill interrupted and yelled out.

"JENN WHAT DID I JUST TELL YOU! Until I investigate a little further I don't want anyone, I mean anyone involved because if this just so happens to be false, it will all fall on me."

"You didn't have to raise your voice like that I was only suggesting," she pouted. He knew how fastidious she could be and he softly apologized. "Apology accepted but I'm totally afraid for you. If this is true that means you're working for a cold-blooded killer. How am I supposed to sleep at night knowing my husband is working for a devilish demon? What am I supposed to do with my life if something happens to you?" sobbed Jenn.

"Honey listen, I love you and for heaven sakes, if something happened to me you will be just fine. Anyone who survives cancer can survive anything. I definitely would advise you to cash in that five hundred-thousand-dollar life insurance policy, pay the bills, and live your life to the fullest," Bill chuckled.

"I don't see anything funny right now."

"I'm just trying to break up this lachrymose moment," smiled Bill. "Listen Jenn don't worry about my safety. I promise you we're not in harm's way. Just allow me to dig a little bit further before I turn this over to the authorities. My main goal here is to do what's right and that's all." She reluctantly agreed, and they finished dinner silently. Bill broke the silence attempting to win her over.

"Do you want to see some of the documented evidence?"

"I sure do," Jenn said sternly.

Bill threw his hands up in the air appearing frustrated.

CHAPTER TWENTY-ONE

Ever since Bill found out about Passion's secret he thoroughly analyzed her behavior at work waiting for the right moment to approach her. She remained exuberant and nice as usual. In his mind he thought if she had enough guts to hire assassins, to label her an expert of deception wasn't too far-fetched.

Today was the day he was ready to approach her with bribery. His conclusion was if Passion became aggressive, he wouldn't hesitate to go straight to the authorities. He didn't know how she would react but was only moments away from finding out.

Three gentle knocks disrupted her stream of thoughts. She stood up and peeked through the door.

"Hey Bill. What's going on?" Bill strolled into her sumptuous office.

"May I have a seat Ms. Veland?"

"Sure, but can you make it quick. Were both up to our ears trying to play catch up from the last two cases. What's on your mind?"

Bill stood up quickly and looked her square in the face.

"Passion fuck you and this got damn job! Would you like to know why?" Passion was stunned by the words that blurted from Bill's mouth. "Answer me you BLACK BITCH!"

160

"Bill! Oh my goodness! What is wrong with you? You're really making me nervous."

"I'm making you nervous huh! I'M MAKING YOUUUUU NERVOUS!" yelled Bill. "I've got you recorded admitting you've hired some assassins and I'm making you nervous." An extreme rush hovered over Passion and she became dizzy. She didn't see this coming.

"Remember when you had that male client in your office screwing your pretty little brain's out? Yeah, I listened to it all. From that moment on I've had a fetish to listen to your moans. By the way your moans drive me crazy. You're such a moaner." Bill laugh out loud followed by a sly grin.

"What do you want from me Bill? I can give you money. I'll set you up for life and".....................

"Shut up bitch!" His aggression made her jump. "I know you have assassins which means my life is at risk right now, but you better listen to me loud and clear. If anything happens to me or my wife, it's over for you. Are you following me?"

"I'm not going to kill anybody Bill what are you"....... Bill interrupted her.

"I said are you following me?"

"Yes, I'm following you."

"Now this is what I want from you. Half a million dollars in cash delivered in three days at a set location. After that I want twenty-five thousand every month. Here's the good part." Bill walked up to Passion and placed his fingertips on her head and began to caress her face whispering softly in her ear. "I want some of that black juicy pussy Passion. I want to see If I can make you moan so whenever you drop off the cash, make sure you arrive without any panties on. Is that understood? DO YOU HEAR ME?" Bill snarled. She leaned back in her chair feeling hopeless and defeated not to mention very nervous.

"I understand with clarity Bill so could you please stop yelling. I don't want anyone to walk in and hear this conversation."

"Well act like it and take them clothes off right now."

"Bill not here in the office. Can we at least get a room?" Passion pleaded with teary eyes.

"I really don't think you understand how much time and effort I've put forth in this investigation. Don't think for one second that I'm the only one who knows about this and if something happens to me or my wife Passion, they are prepared to head straight to the authorities. I suggest you cooperate or lose it all today. So, for the last time. TAKE OFF YOUR GOT DAMN CLOTHES!"

Passion slowly raised her skirt while teardrops slid from her right cheek. He lustfully savored the moment as she reluctantly removed every garment from her body. After she was naked Bill was unsure of what to do next. He roamed his eyes all over her small curvaceous frame. His pants leg began to flood from his erect penis.

"What I need for you to do is put this white dick in your mouth and suck it like you love it. If you do a poor job it will turn me off completely and trust, you don't want me turned off. So you better satisfy me." She walked around the desk and bent down between his legs and felt disgusted from his scent. Although a rush of vomit hung on the edge of her throat she submissively inserted his erect penis into her mouth.

She didn't want to anger him, so she tried to please him the best way she could. Her body was there but her mind was elsewhere as she stared out the window of her office pretending to be somewhere else. Bill enjoyed every minute of it as he leaned back in the chair with his eyes closed tight. While praying for this moment to pass, she thought she observed a shadow in her window, but couldn't stop because she didn't want to slow his erection. The shadow went away but didn't leave Passion's mind as she sucked a little faster to finish the job. A half an hour had passed and finally he grabbed a fistful of her hair and ejaculated all in her face. She closed her eyes and endured the moment with pure hatred. After he was done she grabbed her garments and headed straight for the bathroom that was adjacent to her office.

When she finally came out of the restroom he could tell she had been sobbing as she walked to her desk and sat down. They both stared at one another.

"Such a beautiful woman you are Passion. I don't like when you cry so don't cry around me. As long as I'm pleased, then you have nothing to worry about." She began straightening things on her desk. "Look at me Passion. I've worked for you for years and you cannot tell me that you weren't fully aware of my crush. I held it in and all you did was ignore and overlook me. Hell,

163

you even embarrassed me a time or two with your smooth let downs. So how does it feel to be in submission to someone you're not attracted too?"

"Look Bill, I'd rather be a woman of few words because I don't want you upset with me, so please relieve me of such questions okay?"

"You little whore! You better damn well answer any question I ask of you." Passion observed the evilness in his eyes.

"Well it's definitely hard to be attracted to a guy that's treating me like this."

"Life is a bitch isn't it Passion Lynn Veland. Rated one of America's top female attorney's! One who took the shortcut to success and now is only a few inches away from the bottom," Bill laughed hard. "I can see your pretty little petite self now. Doing life in prison. Surrounded by a bunch of bull daggers and all of them would be fighting for your sweet little chocolate pie. Well I better be heading home. Listen Passion, don't do anything stupid! You hear? Meet me at Starbucks, nine o'clock on Thursday. Have the money with you and be on time."

Passion didn't know what to do and was afraid to tell anyone especially Terry. She knew he wouldn't be able to handle her being Bill's puppet and would kill him without question. It was at this moment she began sobbing thinking about how her grandmother raised her to do the right things in life.

"I allowed the ways of the world to interfere with my dream and I'm so sorry grandma. You taught me better and this is how I repaid you." Passion was sobbing uncontrollably as she dozed off into a deep sleep from exhaustion.

Bill didn't wait long to start torturing Passion. The very next day he presented her with bribery and ordered her to meet him at the hotel. Passion was confused because his official order was three days, but she obeyed him out of fear and handed him the amount of money he requested. Exuberance was no longer a part of her character. Stress, fear, and anxiety was overwhelming her with every passing hour. Everyone who was a part of her life had become worried, including Pierre. She blamed her lethargic look on her heavy workload, but her bagged droopy eyes and disheveled attire told the truth without her saying a word. It was apparent that Passion was not the same.

CHAPTER TWENTY-TWO

Shawn had turned into a drunken drug head that stalked Passion's whereabouts several days throughout the week. Shantae decided that paying him two hundred dollars a day would make it worth his while. They would meet at different hole in the wall motels in East Omaha.

"So what information do you have for me today Mr. Mattox?" asked Shantae.

"Well boss, I couldn't wait to reveal all the craziness I've witnessed these last few days," Shawn paused and took a good look at Shantae.

"First of all, you gotta tell me why you're dressed like you work here, and wearing that blonde wig?

"Well today I felt the need to be more discreet. You haven't told anyone about this discovery of yours, have you?" asked Shantae

"Of course not, but man oh man you're not going to believe this. Guess what the bitch Passion been doing?"

"What!"

"She's been paying folks to kill people, so she can win her cases. The craziest part is, that white man who works for her in her office, you know the white sccretary dudc?"

"Yeah, I'm hip," replied Shantae."

"He's using blackmail on her for sex. Or should I say white mail." They both chuckled.

"Are you serious? Wow! She's more treacherous and lowdown than I suspected," smiled Shantae.

"Same thing I said. That's why I think you should at least pay me a few extra bills. Her ass is dangerous. How about four hundred for the trouble? Then on top of that, she almost busted me a few times while I was hiding on the side of her office window. I can't stand her ass. I rarely use the word hate but I hate that bitch with a passion. I started messing around with her after the trial and I'm still pissed that I left my loyal woman for her manipulative ass. For a while I wanted to kill the bitch myself. Thought I was in love I guess, but she dropped me like a bad habit, and ever since then my life has been hell." Shawn took a swig of his Seagram's Gin and stared out the window.

"No Mr. Mattox, you have no idea what hell feels like, but you'll know real soon," said Shantae as she screwed the silencer onto her nine-millimeter.

"Huh," replied Shawn as his eyes got big observing what he thought was a gun in Shantae's possession.

"Shantae! What you gone do with that?" Shawn's smile quickly turned into a frown.

"Don't move Mr. Mattox."

"What you mean don't move! What da fuck are you doing with that silencer?" yelled Shawn as he stood up with a serious look on his face. "Look, I already know how to use one if that's why you brought it here! Girl what's wrong with you! Point that thing over there."

167

Shantae pointed the gun directly at him. "If you take so much as a baby step, I am going to shoot you dead right where you're standing. Did you ever think that for one second, I had gotten over you killing my husband, step daughter, and her mother in cold blood? HUH?" Shantae yelled.

"So, you just gone kill me and think bad karma won't catch up with you huh?"

"Not the way it has caught up with you. You murdered them in cold blood which caused my husband to take his own life." Shantae could tell he was about to try something so she held the gun steady using both hands.

"I DIDN'T KILL HIM SHANTAE!"

"You may as well have killed him. You're the root cause of his death. He was my best friend and meant the world to me. The only reason Passion got you off was based off that fact that I tried to bribe her. I begged her to drop you as a client and was willing to pay big money to do so. He would've still been alive if you hadn't been so greedy. He was spoon feeding your bitch ass for years and you betrayed him. Turned on him like a pit bull. YOU HAVE NO IDEA WHAT TYPE OF HELL I'VE LIVED IN SINCE I LOSS MY HUSBAND." Shantae's eyes turned red and she started breathing heavy.

"Listen Shantae, I told you I was innocent. You said it yourself. I thought you genuinely believed me. I mean come on man! I can't go out like this," Shawn pouted as his eyes began to water.

"Mr. Mattox, I have stalked you with hatred ever since the last day of your trial. When I saw you at the bar, that wasn't a coincidence! My plan was to kill your filthy drunk worthless ass that same night. Instead, I could tell you didn't have a pot to piss in or a window to throw it out. Basically, I used you as a flunky. How about you say hello to my cousin Marlow, I'm sure you'll meet that child molesting son of bitch in hell.

"Wait!.................SHANTAE!.........PLEASE!" yelled Shawn holding the Gin bottle as a shield in front of his face.

Shantae squeezed off two silent shots at point blank range. He was dead before his body hit the floor.

THE NEXT DAY

Tiara worked as a secretary for Passion on the main floor. Today she woke up playing gospel music feeling blessed and decided to bring Passion lunch.

"Hi Pas!" smiled Tiara. "You've been working so hard lately, and I wanted to show you how much I appreciate all that you've done, so I brought you lunch." Passion didn't look up or stop writing.

"My days could be a lot better Tee thank you."

"Well honestly, I'm kind of worried about you. You seem a little depressed and not to mention you have lost weight. Something just doesn't sit well boo." Passion was still writing with her head down. "Okay I get it, you don't wanna be bothered, but just remember I'm here for you and I love you. Our friendship is unconditional, and you can always talk to me about anything." Tiara kissed Passion on her cheek, put the lunch on her desk and headed towards the door.

"Wait Tiara, please, don't leave. Sit down. Look, I'm as good as I can possibly be right now. Yes, I do have some serious issues going on right now, but it's something I must deal with and overcome. I'll be okay."

"Passion you have my shoulder, loyalty, and everything else and if anyone is hurting you, I'll go to the extreme to remove that person from your life do you hear me?"

Passion observed the genuine care in her eyes and realized that her friendship was for a lifetime. Although Passion initiated their reuniting, she didn't allow her to get too close. Afraid of Tiara's inability to handle only friendship and not lust, was the reason. Suddenly old feelings began emanating as she stared at her childhood friend. Her vulnerability spoke volumes and she desperately needed an ear to listen. More than anything she needed help, advice, and solace and Tiara seemed like the perfect candidate.

"Okay Tiara, I'm in trouble and I have no idea how to get myself out of this mess. Not to mention I feel like I'm always being followed. I feel hopeless and severely overwhelmed to say the least."

"First of all Passion, this look you're wearing is foreign to me. You've always been the strongest woman I know outside of my mom and granny Veland. I mean I understand people get weak sometimes but Pas, you must pick and choose those moments and right now is not the time boo. Pull it together before you lose yourself. Strong women aren't allowed to fail in the fourth quarter with thirty seconds left in the game. We're champions. Didn't you say you was a soldier? Not to mention you've never taken the time to grieve over granny's death. All you did was transition right into your law firm business without giving yourself time to heal. Listen honey, your strength and my strength together equal power!" Tears stung Passions eyes as she smiled at her best friend.

"Let's take the rest of the day off girl we have plenty to talk about," replied Passion.

After hearing what Passion had to say in its entirety, Tiara was enraged for more reasons than one.

"Do you see why I was wearing the look of despair? My life is now on the verge of being destroyed because I decided to go against all of the morals my granny instilled in me." Tears flowed freely down her face as she finished telling her the story.

"First of all, I know you trust me with your life or you would've never revealed this to me. All I wanna know is why? Why did you make such a drastic decision? You were good enough Pas! More than good enough." Passion started pacing back and forth and found herself shaking from anxiety.

"Remember when I endured my first loss in the courtroom? I was what, seven and zero at the time?"

"Yes, I remember," replied Tiara.

"Well I didn't handle that well at all Tee. In fact, I never wanted to experience that feeling again. Accepting a record that was tainted with losses was a fear of mine. I didn't want to be average. I worked too hard for that and to make a long story short, I became addicted to the rush of winning. So, I decided to put together an operation that would make my road to success a tad bit easier and I'm paying for it all right now."

"Tell me this, do you think your grandmother's death played a part in bringing forth such an evil plan? Reason I asked is because if she was still alive, I know none of this would've happened." Passion contemplated her words for a second and began to cry ruefully.

172

"Tiara she's probably turning over in her grave right now," cried Passion.

"Don't think like that because life is far from over. Now we have to figure out what we're going to do to get you out of this mess."

"The assassin job was ceased before this happened with Bill because I was in the process of changing my life. I knew it was time for a soul cleansing and I didn't want any more blood on my hands. Karma showed up and showed out. I guess change wasn't an option?" Passion lowered her chin."

"Hold your head up Passion we're gonna figure this one out. Trust me!

"Tiara please keep this between us. The only thing I can do at this point is remain his puppet and prayerfully he will remain silent and loyal to his word."

"No Passion, we can't allow him to continue taking advantage of you. Let me kill his white ass and then the blood will be on my hands."

"Stop talking like that Tiara. The only reason I told you all of this is because I honestly trust that you'll keep this between us."

"Okay Pas I'll keep my promise but"..............

Tiara was interrupted by the sound of Passion's cell phone.

"Be quiet for a second this is Pierre calling." Passion wiped her face and cleared her throat before she answered. "Hello.......................... okay well I understand and I'm sorry about that. I've been

173

meaning to return your calls, but I've been extremely busy"............ Pierre continued to talk even though Passion tried to cut him off.

"Well hey listen I really hate to cut you off, but I can't talk right now....................yes I still just want to remain friends... but hey can we discuss this later... Pierre! PIERRE I CAN'T TALK RIGHT NOW GOT DAMMIT GOODBYE!" Passion aggressively ended the call and threw her cell phone across the room. "My goodness he's really starting to annoy the hell out of me. I mean seriously. Motherfucker bye!"

Passion sat down and palmed her head with the look of frustration. Tiara walked over and picked up her cell phone and handed it to Passion.

"Well guess what Pas? At least you didn't crack your screen." They both started cracking up laughing.

CHAPTER TWENTY-THREE

"I must admit, I really did miss my best friend."

"Yeah I missed you too Tee. Life was good when our friendship was tight. If we could only turn back the hands of time," Passion started sobbing.

"Pas don't cry. You know what? I suffered all these years we were apart and felt a tremendous amount of guilt for ruining our friendship."

"Well Tee don't focus on the past we're moving forward now and besides look at how both of our lives turned out. We weren't raised like that and I can't believe I allowed the ways of the world to taint my spirit. My granny was a very faith driven woman and she taught me better. You survived your deficit but me on the other hand, I've got a full trial ahead of me. Speaking of trials, your ass went to prison. I could not sip that bottle of wine fast enough after I spoke with your mother that day. What in the world was all that about? Girrrrrrlllll you have got to catch me up on everything. I've been dying to find out about this!"

"Honeyyyyyy! I was in Cleveland getting paid baby!"

"How was Cleveland? Is it extremely busy or is it like Omaha?"

"Actually Pas, I miss 'The Land' as they call it, but don't get it twisted, just like Omaha, beauty plus hustle don't sit well with folks. You know the hatred towards a black woman getting paid is universal. Then you already know that getting a man to look my way has never been a problem. To make a long story short, that guy that I moved up there with was a mess girl. He met some big belly pill popping whore he called himself creeping with. Then he started pillow talking and told her all our business. So, when she found out that he was still living with me she went crazy on his ass. He quit answering her phone calls and she called the police and told them everything. Girl and guess what?"

"What?" Passion asked smiling from ear to hear.

"Once I laid eyes on that whore, I was dead. D.E.A.D. She was only twenty-eight years old and looked like Shaq in a dress. The bitch looked like she wore a size thirteen shoe, her booty was flat with hail damage, and her titties were hanging damn near down to her knees. Wearing dollar store bras and shit. She needed a brazier. Hell, she should've tried out for the Cleveland Browns I believe they would've considered her for a lineman position." Passion giggled out loud.

"Tee you know you still funny as shit, right? Okay so even though I'm scared to ask, how did the guy look?"

"Girl he was fine as hell, but ole girl owned a few child care facilities, breaded up and paid like she weighed honey. He called it a friend with benefits package. Yeah, she came with a package alright. Delivered my ass right inside the Federal Penitentiary ole thirsty heffa." They both laughed.

"No wait Tee you're not saying it right. You gotta say Painataintrie," said Passion. Tiara laughed out loud.

"Honey it was something to remember but I learned my lesson. I'll never cross that path again."

"Well I'm glad you got away from all of that mess."

"Tee I wasn't going to bring this up but since we're speaking on the past, did you catch the breaking news last night on channel five?" Tiara lowered her chin with a sad expression.

"Yeah I know. Shawn was murdered. You know I truly loved that man. I mean I know he's part of the reason our friendship ended, but I would've probably still been with him had you two stopped sleeping around. On top of all that, I knew you didn't like that man. I felt like it was done out of spite."

"Okay! I'll admit that part of it was done out of spite but"........(Passion paused). "I can't lie the sex was good. I mean you knew what you were getting, and you knew what I never had. At the end of the day you had no business pulling that bullshit but that's neither here nor there. Do you miss him?"

"Well not really. Before that situation happen between us we were on shaky grounds anyway. I just wish I could've said goodbye, but that's life. Why did you cut ties with Pierre? He seemed like a really good dude?"

"I'm in love with someone else," smiled Passion.

"Someone like who girl bye you don't know what love is stop it," Tiara chuckled.

"No, I'm serious this time Tee."

"Who is it, do I know him?"

"Nah, actually he's one of my assassins." Tiara's eyes got big.

"That Terry dude you were speaking about earlier? Girl go outside and dig the dirt I'm dead." Tiara shook her head.

"Don't be so dramatic damn."

"Well I see he softens your heart when you speak about him. That's a huge deal right there. On the other hand, I was hoping one day we could rekindle what we had." Tiara began to tear up a little.

"Tee, first of all, we've got to stop all this crying girl." They both laughed. "We'll always be close friends but I'm in love with Terry, which is another reason why I'm so broken. I'm about to lose the love of my life along with the relationship I've built with his beautiful daughter Evelyn. I mean I love that little girl like she's my own. I just can't see my life without them. Everything was going so smooth. Life was good until that monster Mr. Bill started this shit. Girl gross is an understatement. His balls smell like sewer water and I held my breath the entire time. I haven't been able to eat anything because of it. The truth of the matter is, I paid folks to kill for me, but I've never had it in my heart to kill anybody. If I did, that bastard would've been dead. As far as our relationship, I feel blessed to have you here in my presence. Just analyze this situation for a second. Do you realize how alone I would feel right now if I didn't have you to confide in? I know God is real and going forward the only thing I can do is keep asking for forgiveness. Granny used to always say, "God knows your heart Passion." Right now, just by you being here, I feel his presence. Granny was right."

"I agree Pas. Yes, I agree. Okay so you have two assassins, right?"

"Ex assassins, but yes."

"Are you going to bring them out of retirement because something has to be done and fast."

"Well Bill said if he dies, someone has instructions to go straight to the police and I'm not underestimating that man. Just by me orchestrating this entire ordeal as a lawyer, that would land me a lengthy prison sentence. That judge would make an example out of me. I mean that's if he really has me on tape and I'm sure he does because he repeated everything verbatim that Terry and I discussed in my office. Not to mention I'm a black woman! Mess around and give me the damn death penalty."

"Pas you've got to play by his rules, but I got some good prison wisdom from this Mangle."

"Hold on Tee, stop. What's a mangle?"

"A woman who acts like a man in prison."

"Holy shit Tee go ahead and throw some dirt on me I'm dead." They chuckled.

"She said deception and manipulation is the fuel that runs the enemies heart, but lust clears the pathway to his mind."

"Hmmm. Damn that's deep. Gives me something to think about. Okay Mangle I aint mad at ya!" Passion laughed.

"In other words, put it on his ass and make that bastard fall in lust with you."

"I think I just threw up in my throat Tee. The thought of that makes my stomach hurt."

CHAPTER TWENTY-FOUR

Terry and Passion were sound asleep when the vibration from her phone startled her. Afraid she would miss a call she kept it underneath her pillow every night. She instantly grabbed the phone hurrying to the bathroom to talk in private.

"Wake your sexy ass up........Hello," said Bill as he waited for a response. "Hey, you better say something, and fast."

"Bill I just woke up and It took me a second to catch my breath. What's up."

"What the hell you mean what's up! Bring that ass to me asap. I want you to wear a long coat with nothing under it. Not even so much as a thong. Is that clear?" Passion remained silent for a moment after she heard the hostility in his voice.

"You stupid bitch! Are you listening to me?"

"Yes Bill I hear you. Where are you?"

"I'm at the Hilton Hotel in Ralston. It's the only one out here in this area so It shouldn't be hard to find. I'll be waiting in room two-ten." Click. Passion silently wept as she gathered herself preparing to sneak pass Terry who was snoring. She was living what seemed like a nightmare and at times she didn't know how much more she could take. A part of her wanted to reveal all of this to Terry with hopes they could come up with a solution but then again, it could very well be a grave mistake.

Bill opened the door and studied Passion to see if she had worn what he'd instructed.

"What took you so long?"

"I got here as fast as I could Bill. There's so many cops out and that would've been breaking news for them to bust me driving without any clothes on at four in the morning." As she reluctantly sat down on the bed she noticed a plate covered with cocaine and a bottle of Swarovski Alize sitting on the end table. Those items were pricey not to mention Bill spent about two thousand dollars on the Alize.

Passion fire fueled when she thought about how her money was used to buy the hotel alcohol and drugs. Bill sat on the bed with an anxious sly grin and powder remaining on the tip of his nose. Passion was never exposed to this side of him and couldn't be paid to believe this if she didn't see it with her own eyes.

"Take it off," he demanded. She complied. "Now come to daddy baby. I want to taste them chocolate lips." Passion stood and kissed him without an ounce of passion and suddenly he pushed her down on the floor. "You think I can't tell that you hate kissing me? I know my touch disgust you but you better start pretending to like it got dammit. Bill removed his shirt and came out of his boxers. "Get on your knees." She reluctantly went to work. As much as he enjoyed the way she felt, he also enjoyed torturing her and he ejaculated in her mouth. That was something he had never done in any other session causing Passion to spit it to the floor. "You're a stupid dumb whore!" Whop! A blow to the jaw tumbled her over.

"If you spit anything else out, I will kill your ass myself." Passion silently cried as he tortured her soul. He demanded that she turn around and that's when she felt him sodomizing her with aggression as she held on to the couch for dear life praying in secret. After he ejaculated inside her, he sat by the table losing himself in a plate of cocaine. After his short high wore off he yelled, "go home to your nigger boy I'll be in touch."

Terry was in the basement working out when he heard Passion come through the front door. She zoomed straight to the bathroom and poured Epsom salt in the water to soak the soreness away.

"What's up baby! Where did you go this morning?" Passion tried to avoid any eye contact due to the facial swelling from Bill striking her at the hotel. "Passion what is going on with you and why is your face puffy? Terry moved in closer and sat on the side of the tub to make sure what he observed was real. Attempting to touch Passion's face she smacked his hand.

"Please...... don't," said Passion. Terry suspected cheating for a few weeks now but decided to omit his insecure thoughts for the sake of her heavy workload.

"Passion baby look, I need to know what's going on with you. You left this house at wee hours of the morning, then you called yourself trying to zoom pass me, so I couldn't see your face is swollen.

If someone is harming you, I should be the first one to know." Passion kept her head held down.

"For the last few weeks I've been wrecking my brain trying to figure out what I did wrong to cause this sudden change within our vibe. Please talk to me!"

"It's over Terry. I'm sorry it's over and I don't want to discuss why right now I just really need time to myself. I have so much going on and I'm overwhelmed."

"What the hell you mean it's over?" asked Terry using a harsh tone. "So, I'm just supposed to walk away like a chump huh? Hmmm okay! I see the design of your flawed character. You use men until they're no longer needed. What Pas, you found somebody to fuck you better than me?" Passion remained silent.

"I guess he fucked you so good you didn't mind him beating your ass huh."

"GET THE HELL OUT OF HERE RIGHT NOW," yelled Passion as she plunged out of the shower to look him directly in his eyes. Terry grabbed Passion tight after feeling the weakness of her spirit.

"Baby I'm sorry. I love you Pas!.........You're my joy..........Evelyn and I both are equally blessed to have you and we've been happy ever since you embraced us. Baby listen to me, whatever it is we can talk about it. Please don't push us away." Passion cried in Terry's arms.

"Terry, I just can't do this with you right now. I'm sorry........ I can't." Terry pulled away slowly and kissed her on her forehead.

"Right now Pas, I believe that there's much more going on in your life than I thought. So, with that said, respectfully I'll give you all the time you need. Just know that I love you and always will." Terry grabbed his coat and slowly walked towards the front door. "I'll come get the rest of my things while you're at work." Soon as Terry closed the door all Passion could do was weep.

"God please help me.........Please Help me.........I'm sorry. I'm so sorry."

CHAPTER TWENTY-FIVE

Jennifer opened the door for the private investigator. "You must be Mr. Wells?"

"Yes ma'am and you must be Jennifer," said Mr. Wells as they shook hands.

"Well come on in. May I offer you something to drink?"

"No thank you."

"Well you can have a seat right there while I go grab my cup of coffee." Mr. Wells glanced at the wall of portraits before making his way to the dining room table. Jennifer quickly grabbed her coffee and sat down.

"I'm going to start off by giving you a brief introduction of what to expect along with a form you must sign if you decide to render services today. I've been in business for approximately twenty years and nothing will be discussed over the phone other than a simple confirmation of any upcoming meetings. I will be taking notes during this meeting today. Is that okay Mrs.... I didn't catch your last name."

"Oh, how rude of me. My full name is Jennifer Picalo and yes you can take whatever notes you like."

"Ok Mrs. Picalo, my retainer's fee is two hundred and fifty dollars, which is nothing more than a fee for any wasted time if you decide to cancel my services. If and when you decide to continue, I charge seventy-five dollars per hour. That can be a bit pricey depending upon the amount of time you book me for. Is that something you can afford Mrs. Picalo?"

"Yes sir and besides I heard you were the best."

"Well let's get down to the nitty gritty. First things first, please be direct and specific in detail."

"Well lately I've noticed a dramatic change in my husband's demeanor and I need to know what's going on. Since you said be direct, I believe my husband is cheating. Plain and simple. He lost his job a few months ago and has been showering me with these expensive gifts. Things we couldn't afford with both of our salaries put together. He sneaks out the back door at wee hours of the morning and says he's working at another Law firm office for private pay. He claims this job requires him to start at four a.m. A few times he's stayed out all night and when I confront him about it all, he says he's putting together a brighter future for us. I just don't know what to say. My brother is a Police Officer, but I didn't want to involve him because Bill and I vowed to keep our business away from family. I figured hiring you was the only way I could find out the truth."

"Tell me something Jenn, May I call you that"?

"Yes, please."

"Do you suspect any substance abuse or narcotic use of any kind may possibly be occurring?"

"Actually, that came to mind but being I have so many drug users on my father side of the family, he hasn't displayed any drug user behaviors. He doesn't lash out at me or sleep for days. He appears happy and energetic. Well, unless he's taking uppers!"

"Okay here is what I need for you to do. Jot down everything you see and hear from him in the next twenty-four hours. Question his whereabouts and finances. He may become uneasy, but the goal is to make him blurt out things that may not seem to be of any substance to you, but valuable to this investigation. Give me a call when you're done, and we can meet up at a time that's convenient for you. How does the McDonalds on Broadway street sound for our meeting destination?"

"You mean the one in Council Bluffs, right?"

"Yes. I'll meet you there when you're ready."

"That will be great Mr. Wells. Here's your check and a picture of my husband sir."

"Okay great! You have a great day Jenn."

LATER THAT EVENING

Mariah hadn't heard from Terry for a few days after he confided in her about how Passion wanted to end their relationship. Concerned that he would relapse, she decided to go out looking for him. Ironically today was also her deceased daughter's birthday and she wanted to share a cocktail with Terry. She knew he would listen attentively.

"I need a stiff drink right about now. Terry where the hell are you?" Mariah mumbled to herself while pulling into the liquor store.

"I'll take that fifth of Christian Brothers, two cups of ice, and a pack of Newport shorts in a box please. After popping in the late Tupac c.d., she began to sip her drank and reminisce about her daughter. As tears began to cloud her vision, she decided to park at Carter Lake. She called Passion and Terry back to back and received no answer. "Dang on voicemail. I guess I'll leave a message. Hi Passion, I've been trying to reach you to see if you know where Terry is. Would you please call me back as soon as you receive this message? Thank you. Holy shit I have to pee."

Mariah left her car running while she jogged to the outhouse to release herself.

"Oh my goodness this feel so good." Mariah started laughing at how fast she had gotten drunk. "Fuck I hope I can make it home. I am seriously intoxicated. Terry, where are you? While slowly walking back to her vehicle, she observed a light skinned young lady

189

leaning on her car which made her walk a little faster. "Can I help you?"

"Why do you want to help me," asked the lady.

"Well first of all, you're leaning on my got damn car. Do I know you?"

"No, you don't know me at all, but your boss does."

"My boss? I think you got me confused with someone else."

"Nah, I know exactly who you are. Trust me."

"Trust you? Look, why are you messing with me lady? Today is my daughter's birthday and I'm just trying to sip a little bit and chill, so I really don't know why you're leaning on my car, but I would appreciate it if you would remove yourself away from my vehicle and I'm saying this politely as I can."

Mariah hopped inside her car and attempted to start the ignition but realized her keys were missing.

"What the fuck! What the hell did I do with my keys? Damn I sure hope I didn't leave them in that outhouse or drop them while I was running. Dammit I'm too drunk for this shit." Mariah didn't realize the lady started to walk away.

"Excuse me miss have you seen any keys? Excuse me. Excuse me." The lady kept walking. "Stupid bitch," said Mariah. Mariah was interrupted with a loud growl.

"No bitch you are not excused. Maybe your keys are buried inside of your daughter's grave. The daughter you killed! Yeah, I guess I don't seem like a stupid bitch after all do I?" Mariah eyes were about to pop out of her head as she dropped her full cup of Christian Brothers on the ground.

"What the hell you on? What is all this about and how dare you speak my daughter's name bitch you don't know me for real. Aa a matter of fact, you don't know me at all. If you did you would know that I will beat the fuck out of you. Don't do me!" yelled Mariah as she walked towards the out-house looking for her keys. She opened the door in a hurry and grabbed for her cell phone shakily and nervous unaware that this lady was following right behind her. Terry's voicemail came on.

"Terry, this crazy ass bitch is following me and I'm drunk, scared and this hoe really needs Jesus Terry. She's talking all crazy and I don't have my gun with me or nothing man can you please..............damn! My phone went dead! Are you fucking serious!"

Mariah slowly opened the door to the outhouse and there standing was this woman holding her keys in her hand.

"Bitch! Give me my fucking keys."

"This is for your daughter on her birthday. Not to mention all those people you have murdered in cold blood. YOU HEARTLESS BITCH!"

The lady shot Mariah at point blank range leaving a hole in her forehead the size of a quarter.

CHAPTER TWENTY-SIX

Terry had never contemplated using drugs again until Passion ended their relationship. Although their relationship was brief, he had fell in love very quickly. Unable to dissect what happened between them, he became engulfed with grief. Heroine was the only medicine that could numb his pain of defeat and he quickly called his guy and purchased a few grams.

As he waited for him to arrive, thoughts of Passion penetrated his mind. He felt like a simpleton for believing that she'd loved him. Terry was truly convinced that she was his soul mate until reality revealed its ugly face. Even though he knew he had to overcome his anguish, right now it felt almost impossible. After his heroine connect came and went, there he sat looking down at the table staring the drugs face to face.

"This one's for you Passion." He snorted a line and sat back on the couch feeling like he was on top of the world. Grabbing his cigarettes to keep his high awake he felt a warm sensation that made him smile, but it was momentary. He then went for another line. Suddenly the euphoria made him stand up and feel like he was on top of the world.

"Damn! I forgot how good this shit made me feel! Passion who?"

He let out a loud laugh and turned on his new E-40 cd. He started dancing around and suddenly noticed there was breaking news on the television. He turned down his music and tuned in.

'Mariah Thomas was killed in cold blood at Carter Lake.'

Terry thought he was dreaming and sat down briefly. Then he got back up again when he observed her picture flash across the screen which was his confirmation.

"Mariahhhh!........Mariahhhh!" he yelled with rage causing his high to quickly disperse. Grabbing his phone, he called Passion several times but every single time, her voicemail came on.

"I'm gone find out who did this Mariah! This is war no doubt Fam! I'm going all out for you!" He snorted the rest of his lines, hopped in his car, and drove around to calm down the overwhelming grief that surrounded him. When he stopped at the stop sign, he suddenly felt his heart beating faster than usual and broke out in a sweat. He then felt the presence of an ice-cold rush that caused his foot to lay off the gas.

Unable to control his muscles he crashed into the curb causing other cars around him to stop to see if he needed help. Terry was unresponsive. An onlooker yelled out, "Sir are you ok? Are you ok sir?" Terry was convulsing which made this person call nine one-one.

****

As time passed Bill continued to use Passion as a sex slave. Passion knew it was only so much more of this she could put up with. Every day she would brainstorm ways she could remove herself from this situation. Tiara suggested torture, but Passion knew that tenacity would play its part. She knew Bill enjoyed this so much that he'd die saying he had a copy of her recorded confessions. She also knew that the person who had a copy was not his wife, since he recently contemplated killing her, so they could be together more openly. As she continued to pretend to fall deeper in love with him his aggression towards her began to melt away.

Passion realized the eloquence she had over him and knew that cooperation was the only key to freedom. She decided to play him like a game of poker.

Private investigator Wells studied Bills movements for a few weeks. He gathered more than enough evidence by snapping pictures of them together at Passion's bungalow and at different hotels. The most vivid picture was at Bill's hideaway nest haven he'd secretly purchased located on the outskirts of the city.

Bill enjoyed watching Passion stand naked in front of the bay window while admiring the way her chocolate skin glistened in the sunlight.

Mr. Wells was a tad bit fascinated with Passions physique and also tickled pink about how easy it was to see right inside of the bay window. Amazed by the amount of cocaine, alcohol and hard-core sex he observed, yet concerned about a gray Lexus parked outside of both Passion and Jennifer's house on three separate occasions. All three times he was unable to make out the identity of this person who wore all black and kept their head down.

He speculated that Jennifer had possibly hired someone else to investigate, but to avoid blowing his cover, he kept his mind focused on what he was hired to do. Stalk Bill.

CHAPTER TWENTY-SEVEN

Jennifer sat at home anxiously waiting on the information regarding her husband when a knock at the door caused her stomach to have butterflies. She knew that Mr. Wells was about to reveal her husband's deceit and wasn't sure if she was mentally prepared for the bad news. Jennifer slowly opened the door.

"Hey Mr. Wells, I've been waiting for you. Come on in."

"Hey Jenn. I gathered as much information as I could, so have a seat so I can show you what I've managed to put together." He opened his small briefcase and handed Jenn several pictures. "Some of these photos are disturbing to say the least but before I explain anything to you, I would rather you observe them all."

Mr. Wells did not interrupt her thoughts as she studied each photo in silence. He knew that what she was observing would bring forth pain, betrayal, and fear, but his job description excluded the ability to provide solace. Jennifer broke down and started crying before she could finish looking through the whole stack of pictures.

"This is his boss! Why would he do this to me? To us! We've been together through the thick, thin, good and bad. To make matters even worse, it's with a black woman.

"A beautiful educated famous black woman," Mr. Wells thought to himself.

"Okay Mr. Wells I'm ready to hear whatever it is you would like to add regarding this investigation."

"He's definitely abusing narcotics."

"I'm sorry I just can't believe that for one second Mr. Wells. I must see that with my own two eyes. I mean that is just too"......

Mr. wells interrupted.

"Here you go. Look at this picture right here Jenn. At a glance, this picture may appear meaningless, but if you look closely you'll see that your husband is buying drugs from this guy. Now since I knew that you would be in denial about his drug usage, I saved this picture for that reason alone." Jennifer stared at the picture and the tears began to flow.

It was Bill doing a line of cocaine while Passion stood by his side butt naked.

"Wow this is too much for me to take in," cried Jennifer.

"Mrs. Picalo, my job here is complete but if you ever need me again, I'm only a phone call away."

"Thank you for your assistance sir. Here's your final payment. I'll be okay. I mean I paid you for a reason and I guess I was hoping my assumptions were false, nevertheless you have a great day sir." After he left she laid on the sofa ruminating over his infidelity.

Jennifer decided it was best not to disclose anything to her husband for a while for safety reasons. In deep thought about the pain from her past brought forth a depression and played a huge part in her turning into a lightweight alcoholic. Bill was naive and thought maybe her cancer was slowly returning.

Jennifer was tired of crying. For the last two weeks her emotions were all over the place. She tried on a few outfits, but they were too big from skipping meals several times throughout the week. She made her best effort to motivate herself as much as she could to go outside and enjoy some of the sunshine and breeze that the morning news boasted about earlier that morning.

Jennifer grabbed her case of Budweiser and sat on the back patio staring into the sky as the wind blew listening to Shania Twain. Although the sun was shining, the dilapidation of her marriage had left her feeling gloomy.

"How could he do this to me. Son of a bitch! I don't think a man on the street would've treated me this way." Jennifer observed a gray Lexus parked across the alley way. "Why is that car parked like that? Never mind! I guess I'm turning into the nosy neighbor." Jennifer busted out laughing. While bending down to grab another beer a strange voice startled her.

"Excuse me ma'am, I'm sorry to scare you but." Jennifer interrupted.

"You scared the dickens out of me and why are you back here in my yard?"

"I'm so sorry I didn't mean to scare you. I'm looking for my little puppy. My daughter took her out walking about forty-five minutes ago and somehow, she got away. I've been on a hunt for my poochie ever since. I was just wondering have you seen a little Yorkshire Terrier? She's all white with a blue ribbon tied to her tail?"

"Oh no honey I'm sorry I haven't seen any dogs at all around here. May I ask what's her name?"

"Her name is Calais." This lady observed tears in Jennifer's eyes.

"I'm sorry to ask ma'am but are you okay?" Jennifer began to cry.

"No, I'm not. I'm messed up and my emotions are running wild. I feel like I'm in menopause or something."

"Well do you mind if I give you a hug." The lady quickly hugged her tightly.

"You're such a nice lady. I hope you find your puppy. I know I shouldn't be crying in front of a stranger, but I guess it is what it is. My mother always told me pain is universal."

"Yes, and I'm a woman first ma'am."

"I guess you're right. Well hey, have a beer. Maybe you need something to help you relax while you search for Calais."

"I'm not a beer drinker but thanks for offering."

"How about a glass of wine, I have plenty to choose from."

"Well, I'll take a small glass of wine." Jennifer brought this lady in the kitchen. Look behind that bar over there and pick out which one you prefer, and I'll grab the corkscrew. You're welcome to have a seat."

"Well I really should be out looking for my pooch and I don't wanna seem like a moocher."

"No, I insist. I feel like you're a blessing. I needed a hug and God sent you to me, so this is the least I can do. What's your name?"

"My name is Shonda."

"That's a beautiful name. Well my name is Jenn." Shonda observed the family photos on the wall.

"Any children?"

"No kids just a husband who's a freaking adulterer."

"Well you're a beautiful lady and I can tell you have a kind heart, so karma will haunt him forever. Don't sit here crying and blaming yourself. As long as you know you have done the best you could've done for your marriage then, don't worry. Things will brighten up soon. I'm sure you're hurting, but time heals all wounds," smiled Shonda. Well Jenn I better get going. Shonda started walking towards the door when Jenn yelled out.

"He cheated on me with a black woman! A beautiful black woman. He lied and told me he had some type of video and is gathering evidence, so he can turn it over to the police, but I hired a private investigator. That lying bastard is sleeping with her."

"Oh my goodness Mrs. Jennifer, I'm so sorry to hear that. Did you see the video?"

"Hell no and I've asked to listen to the audio, but he says it's top secret. He's a liar and I just pray that God will have mercy on his soul. He's one sick son of a bitch. Shonda I'm sorry I had to vent to somebody."

"Oh no ma'am I totally understand. I hate that I have to leave you, but I'll keep you in my prayers. Don't worry honey he'll get what's coming to him."

"Thanks sweetie. I hope you find Calais. Let's exchange numbers just in case I see her then I can call you."

"Okay and thank you so much Jenn. You have such great hospitality." Jennifer watched Shonda walk across the street and climb into her gray Lexus as she sat back on the patio with her wine and beer, feeling a momentary sense of relief.

CHAPTER TWENTY-EIGHT

Passion was busy at the office cleaning up when she received a call from Tiara.

"Hey Tee, what's going on?"

"Hey Pas! My mother just called and told me that my father was sick. I have to book an immediate flight to St Louis Missouri tomorrow."

"Oh no! Are you okay?"

"Yeah, I'm fine, I just pray it's not life threatening. We haven't repaired the pieces that were broken between us since I was a teenager. He's been diagnosed with some type of cancer, and I'm just worried."

"Well do you need any help with the financial aspect of this trip? You know I got ya back boo."

"Thanks Pas, I'm fine. I've been saving my cash plus you've done so much for me already. I'll call you when I come back."

"Take all the time you need honey; this job will be here when you get back."

"Thank you, Pas! You're the best!"

****

The doorbell broke Jennifer's rueful reverie. Anticipating her brother's arrival her nerves were getting the best of her and she didn't reveal any specifics but stressed to him it was a matter of life or death. An active police officer for twelve years, those words along with the worry in his sister's voice had him on the edge. She opened the door.

"Oh Donnie," she cried and fell into his arms.

"I came as fast as I could. I decided to stop and grab us both some fresh coffee."

"Great call brother!"

"I figured you needed some caffeine." Jenn had her head down still in shock blocking the door.

"Sis don't just stand there let me in and tell me what's going on." Jennifer cried through her nose uncontrollably.

"I'm sorry Don. Come on in and have a seat. I'm just so shook up."

"Well Jenn, whatever it is, I'm sure it will be ok. Please calm down."

She reluctantly nodded in his arms as they slowly sat together on the sofa. Jennifer sipped her coffee.

"It's Bill. He's having an affair with his boss. What's ironic is that he accused her of being a part of some corruption."

"What kind of corruption are we talking about here Jenn?"

Jennifer told Donnie everything. What aroused him were the files that Bill showed her of various unsolved homicides that actuated inside of several cases that Passion had just so happened to be a part of.

"Are those files still here?"

"I don't think so. I searched this house thoroughly and couldn't find anything. Not even one loose page."

"How about we search one more time sis." They rummaged through the house, but no files were found. He grabbed her by the shoulders.

"Listen to me loud and clear Jenn! Bill may be involved more than we think. His affair indicates either he's involved or blackmailing her for his sexual pleasures." Jennifer covered her mouth and began to weep.

"We've been married for twelve years Donnie why would he throw it all away for an evil woman like her. Brother I could kill that man with my bare hands." Donnie observed her bottom lip quivering uncontrollably.

"Jenn I can't answer that, but I guarantee he'll pay for this, and that goes for all the parties who we're involved."

Donnie immediately went to his boss with the information and the spark instantly caught a flame.

F.B.I. was quickly notified due to the enormity crimes in different states. Although there was no solid concrete evidence against Passion, a silent investigation had emanated into existence.

CHAPTER TWENTY-NINE

Tiara circled the block a few times before parking down the street from Jennifer's place. She observed that the time read ten thirty-six on her watch as she took a few deep breaths and gulped a shot of Seagram's Gin to calm her nerves. Then she grabbed the duffel bag from her back seat and made her way to her front door. Jennifer was expecting her arrival. Tiara called her earlier confirming the death of her puppy stating she was run over by a car. Jennifer displayed her condolences and invited her over for some drinks.

So far Tiara's plan was moving along in the right direction. Instead of ringing the doorbell she called her on an Obama phone to let her know she was at her front door.

"Hey girl I'm glad you made it. Come in! I was worried about you. Two years ago, I lost my precious puppy and I was devastated," said Jennifer. Tiara walked inside, and Jennifer noticed the bag she was carrying.

"What's in the bag?"

"Oh just a few keepsakes I wanted to show you."

"How sweet! Make yourself comfortable and I'll be right back. Going to run in here and grab us some wine."

"Okay great! While you're doing that I'll go use your restroom. Seem like my bladder is about to bust."

"Oh sure! It's the last door on the right."

Jennifer returned with the wine and noticed ten minutes had passed.

"Shonda are you okay in there?" Tiara didn't answer. Jennifer walked towards the restroom and stopped abruptly due to the knife pointed at her throat. Jennifer dropped the glass of wine.

"Scream you little dumb bitch and I will slice your fucking neck off do you understand me?" Jennifer skittishly nodded. Tiara walked her to the chair in the bedroom and made her sit.

"Tie your feet together and tie them extremely tight. DO IT NOW!" She grabbed the rope and obeyed the order.

"When was the last time you talked to your piece of shit ass husband?"

"I haven't talked to him at all today."

"Well what I need for you to do is call him right now and tell him you have an emergency, so he can come home. I don't care how you tell him or what you have to say, just remember your life depends on it."

"Shonda, why are you doing this to me. I thought we were friends." Tiara started pacing and ignoring her questions.

"I'm innocent and whatever he's into I'm not involved so please don't hurt me." Tiara allowed her to keep talking while she grabbed another piece of rope from her bag and tied her torso to the chair.

"Listen lady, as long as you cooperate, you'll live. Go ahead and call him like I asked you to do. You wanna live right?" Tiara handed Jenn her cell phone. Bill answered.

"Hey Jenn," answered Bill.

"I need you to come home right now it's an emergency."

"Well what's the matter honey."

"I'm just feeling really down right now and besides I haven't seen you for hours."

"Well honey you know I'm handling business right now, is this something that could wait?"

"ABSOLUTELY NOT!" yelled Jenn. "Everything in my life is in shambles and it seems as though you could care less." Bill was silent. "Bill If you can't come home then I guess I'll just call my brother and tell him how I feel."

"NO! JENN LISTEN. I'M ON MY WAY. I'll be there shortly." Approximately twenty minutes later, both women heard Bill's car pulling into the garage.

Tiara had her high voltage stun gun tucked inside her jeans ready for his entrance.

"Jenn, I'm home! Where are you?"

"I'm in the back." Bill walked slowly to the room and noticed Jenn tied to a chair and rushed over close to her. Tiara stepped out of the closet and without hesitation charged him furiously sending a high voltage of electricity throughout his body causing him to become indefensible. Bill dropped to the floor like a sack of potatoes. Only thing he could do was accept the tortuous pain while she zapped him three times back to back. She electrocuted him longer than planned due to the pain he inflicted on Passion but didn't want to kill him just yet. Jennifer started screaming.

"Please don't hurt my husband." Jennifer begged.

"YOUR HUSBAND! YOUR HUSBAND! Look at all the mess your bitch ass husband involved you in. You sound like a damn fool right now." Tiara quickly grabbed the rest of the rope from her bag and tied his legs and torso to the bed. Bill was still in shock but able to start mumbling. Although he was slightly disoriented he noticed it was Tiara who shocked him.

"Tiara, is that you? What...... what are you doing here? What the hell is your problem and why am I tied up?"

"Oh Bill! Really? Let's not play dumb here. You know exactly why I'm here. Don't play retarded now you ole worthless manipulative cunt," yelled Tiara. Jennifer looked confused.

"Tiara? Tiara who? I thought your name was Shonda?"

"Listen babe don't say another word. I know exactly who she is. I worked with her at the law Firm." Tiara began pulling out tortuous tools, sitting them on the table. "Look Tiara I can explain everything to you. I mean I also have a few thousand saved up in the bank. Whatever you need me to do, I'll do it. Just please don't hurt us," Bill pleaded.

"Ok, I get it. You're referring to that money you blackmailed from Passion, right? Nah I don't think so Billy Bob. Matter of fact, I don't wanna hear you beg at all bitch." Tiara laughed while she stuffed both of their mouths with socks. Bill frantically tried to wiggle himself loose from the rope. Tiara grabbed a hammer and sat on his thighs facing his feet.

"Mr. Bill? Guess what? That woman you're calling yourself blackmailing and raping is a woman who is very dear to me. Nobody, I mean nobody fucks with her. You picked the wrong one nigga."

She instantly slammed the fork end of the hammer into his shin. The hammer was temporarily stuck. She managed to yank it free. Bill's muffled scream was grueling, and Jennifer cried while watching in horror.

"There's a few things you need to tell me such as who has the recorded information?" Without another word she slammed the hammer into the opposite shin. "Are you ready to tell me?" His merciful sobs ignited her anger. She turned around and put her face to his. "You've got some nerve crying like a little bitch after all the shit you put my friend through. Not even Jesus can you hear you cry you old sick bastard." Tiara got up and grabbed the stun gun off the table, looked down at his wounded legs, and sent another volt through each leg one at a time. Jennifer could not watch. Tiara looked at Jennifer. "Why are you crying? This man doesn't give a damn about you." She snatched the sock from his mouth. "WHO HAS THE WIRE?" Bill slurred his words out as loud as he could.

"There is only one copy I swear. I have it inside my car."

"WHERE AT?" yelled Tiara.

"Inside my glove compartment. Please go get it. You're killing me, and I can't move my legs."

"Fuck your legs. Who has the duplicate?"

"I lied. I made it all up. No one else knows only my wife."

She stuffed his mouth again and grabbed the hunting knife from her bag. She began to aggressively slice his legs seesaw style then poured vinegar all over the wounds. Bill couldn't believe a pain like this had even existed and pleaded with God to make it go away.

"Shouldn't you be talking to the devil? Are you ready to die yet? A man without legs isn't a man at all in my book. Hmmm you're just a worthless piece of shit if you ask me. NOW TELL ME WHAT I NEED TO KNOW, OR I WILL TORTURE YOU UNTIL YOUR LAST BREATH!!!" She snatched the sock from his mouth.

"I swear, I swear, I swear, no one else knows." Tiara stared at him for a moment then walked behind Jennifer, yanked her head back by her hair, placing the knife to her throat.

"Tell the truth or this dumb bitch will die."

"Please don't hurt my wife. I've been completely honest about it all," cried Bill.

"Why did you choose a man like this Jennifer? All these years you mean to tell me you never knew that your so-called husband was a conniving scheming perverted son of a bitch who had a fetish for black women. I may burn in hell for this, but I have no choice." She sliced her throat from ear to ear causing

Bill to wale loudly. At that moment he remembered his love for her and the sight of her death crushed him. He once again tried to wiggle from the rope, but Tiara kicked him in the face and began plunging the knife into his chest ferociously. When she was done with Bill, he was merely recognizable.

CHAPTER THIRTY

Passion was at home relaxing while watching a movie. It was the first time in a while she hadn't heard from Bill all day and felt a sense of peace. Out of the blue her telephone rung and to her surprise it was Terry.

"TERRY! How are you?" said Passion with excitement.

"Not so good Passion. I'm laid up in this hospital bed right now as we speak. I've been here a few days now." Passion fell off the couch trying to sit up.

"Wait, what do you mean a few days. Why haven't you called me and what happened?"

"Right now, there's a lot going on. I prefer not to talk on these phones Pas, so If you wanna holla at me I'm at the county."

"What County?"

"Douglas County Hospital downtown on Woolworth in room two eleven." Passion already had her shoes on and was looking for her jacket.

"I'm on my way."

"Okay I'll see you when you get here then."

"Terry........ I'm sorry about everything and I will explain it all to you when I get there. Soon it will all make sense."

"Well we'll talk Pas, Okay?"

When she walked into his room she noticed his weight decreased and he appeared lethargic. Passion rushed over to him and kissed him on the cheek.

"Didn't think your presence would make ya boy's heart smile but man was I was wrong" Terry admitted.

"Terry, I love you. I never wanted to hurt you, never. Just remember that. Right now, things in my life are so complicated and out of control. Bottom line is everything I did was only to protect us."

"Protect us from what Passion? I'm confused!" Terry seemed frustrated. She held her head down. Terry sensed that something was far more wrong than he expected. "Look baby, explain to me right here and now, what happened to us and why. Don't you think I deserve the truth?"

"Yes, but I had to protect us. Our lives were at stake baby." Terry didn't know what to say but felt a sudden ominous fear in his chest after a lingering silence.

"You mean us as in you and I, or you, I, and Mariah?"

"I mean all of us."

"Mariah is dead Passion. She was killed the night I came here. I saw it on the news and that's part of the reason I landed a bed in this joint. After I caught the news I jumped in my car chasing the wind to release my emotions and crashed into a tree." Passion covered her mouth as tears flooded her eyes.

"Yeah, it's crazy, and what's even worse is, I don't have a clue as to who did it or why she was killed. I'm hurting bad Pas. She was a true friend to me." His voiced cracked as he began to cry. Passion couldn't believe her ears.

"Terry I'm so sorry, but Why? she questioned rhetorically."

"I don't know why. All I know is she was shot in the head at Carter Lake." Passion couldn't hold her tears back any longer.

"Damn Terry I didn't expect to hear this today," she sobbed. Terrys' frustration increased.

"I think it's about time you tell me everything that's going on because right now this shit you are talking about is starting to piss me off. For one you up here talking in codes, just spit the shit out. Then on top of all that my sister from another mother is dead and gone but your sitting up here telling me you have to protect us. FROM WHO?" Terry yelled.

"Somebody that knows everything Terry. That's all I can say until you're out of here."

"WHAT THE FUCK IS GOING ON!! Stop playing with me and matter of fact, I'm not in the mood for this conversation right now. NOT AT ALL!"

"No no no no please calm down. Don't lose it on me. I have everything under control."

"You mean to tell me somebody done found out about our business ventures?" Terry frantically whispered. Passion nodded her head yes.

"Got damn Pas, how did that happen?"

"I was deceived in the worst way, but listen Terry when are you leaving here?"

"I DON'T KNOW!"

"Terry please just listen to me okay!" Terry had a stern look on his face that quickly changed when he observed her nervousness. "What has the doctor diagnosed you with?"

"What you mean diagnosed?"

"I mean do you have any fractures or severe injuries because they may require therapy before you leave."

"I was under the influence when I crashed, so truthfully I'm not sure what these people gone say. All I know is I'm ready to get the hell out of here. That particular day I was upset about us and the reality of her death along with me being high as hell off heroin was too much for my brain to endure and I.....I lost control."

"Oh no! You were using drugs?"

"Actually, it was a habit that I kicked in the past but I picked it back up after we broke up."

Passion eyes were big as she wiped the tears streaming down her cheeks. All she could do was cry while he told his story.

"Don't guilt trip about it though. It's not your fault at all. I was just hurting. I hate myself for that relapse. I thought I was stronger than that addiction. Apparently not."

Although it was painful to reveal, he disclosed everything. He spoke about his drug history and how Mariah assisted him in kicking the habit. All of this information was new to Passion.

"Sorry for causing you to back track down that road again. I never intended to hurt you in any shape, form, or fashion. Will you forgive me?"

"Pas baby listen, I love you, but I need you to always be open and honest with me about everything. You were willing to crash our relationship for the sake of a secret. That don't make sense or add up at all. I should be able to trust my lady at all cost!"

"Yes, your right babe and I promise from here on out, no more secrets. If rehab is what you need, we'll hire the best help possible. I'll never leave your side again," cried Passion.

"Seeing you right now is all the therapy I need for real baby. Missing you made this situation seem like the end of the world. As long as I have my Passion back a rehab facility won't be necessary. Take me home baby," said Terry smiling from ear to ear.

"Well not so fast boo! Can we at least see what the doctor has to say? We got to dot our I's and cross our T''s by making sure you're healthy enough to come home." Terry and Passion held hands until Terry drifted off to sleep.

****

Tiara left the murder scene confident that there was no further threat to Passion and no one else had any copies of the conversation. Still in shock about what took place she decided it was time for a stiff drink. After abolishing her tracks and disposing the weapons, she stopped at the store to grab her a bottle of wine. Although she was anxious to reveal everything to Passion, she decided to wait until she cleansed her body and had a nap. She soaked in a hot bubble bath and sipped her wine laughing at Bill's plea.

"White boy had the nerve to beg and plead for his life after what he just put my sister through. The nerve of you. Pas, you're going to love me for life when you find out these details baby."

After resting well throughout the night, she opened her eyes and immediately called Passion.

"Good morning!"

"Hey good morning Tee. How was your flight?"

"Actually, I didn't go."

"I thought your father was sick. Wait, was it financial because I told you I had your back?"

"Well I'd rather not talk about this over the phone, but we really need to talk. What's a good time to come by?"

"So, you're telling me you never left town?"

"PAS DAMN! We can talk when I get there!"

"Okay! Why are you yelling Tee? Any way you can just come over right now because I still have a few hours before I have to be at the office."

"Okay I'm on my way."

Passion detected skittish behavior when she walked through the door.

"Are you hungry Tee?"

"No!"

"You seem worried what's wrong?" asked Passion. Tiara exhaled.

"Look, I'm just gone be straight up honest about everything. I lied to you."

"Lied about what?" Passion asked curiously.

"About my father being sick and flying out to be with him."

"That's childish as hell and nothing to play with for real. If you wanted the time off all you had to do was request it off in advance. I mean why Lie?"

"That wasn't the case at all Pas."

"Now you're starting to frustrate me. Stop ducking and dodging the issue, I have way too much shit on my plate to be going back and forth with you right now. My babe is in the hospital and I just can't do this with you today."

"I killed him for you......I killed Bill and his wife." Passion spit out her Pepsi.

"What do you mean you killed them. Is this a joke?"

"Would I joke about something so serious?"

"Girl I think you're losing your mind."

Tiara unraveled everything. Passion listened in disbelief as Tiara explained how Jennifer pretended to be distressed and Bill rushed home to a trap. Suddenly Passion realized that Bill didn't make any contact last night or this morning and this was unusual. Passion didn't interrupt her as she continued to spill the beans.

"I tortured his ass Passion and he swore up and down that he was the only one who had the copy of that conversation. Jennifer was genuine, God rest her soul, but she told me that he never allowed her to listen to it." Tiara pulled out the recorded tape and handed it to Passion. "We're safe babe. We're finally safe."

Passion was stunned and was momentarily unable to find her voice.

"What if there's someone out there that has a copy Tee? Do you know my life would be over?"

"Pas listen...The way I tortured his ass, I believed what he said. The man was crying out and pleading for his life. Trust me on this one." Passion dropped her face in the palm of her hands.

"THIS IS MY LIFE TEE!" yelled Passion.

"See, this is why I didn't tell you my plans because I knew you would totally be against it, but at the end of the day......Everything is everything."

"Another thing, do you realize you have committed murder?"

"I know what I did was wrong, but I did it for us. Bill was destroying you and trying to bring down everything you worked so hard for and I just couldn't stand there and allow that to happen. When you hurt, I hurt."

If Passion didn't know Tiara's love was profound, she knew now. They cried in one another arms until they felt restored with strength.

"We're gonna be okay Pas. We're gonna be okay." Tiara promised.

CHAPTER THIRTY-ONE

Tiara left Passion's house with another mission on her agenda. Through Passion she discovered Terry was at the Douglas County Hospital. If it was left up to her he would die in that hospital bed and she was determined to make that happen. After doing some research on the computer about poison, Tiara decided to put a plan into action that would prevent Passion from reconciling with Terry ever again. After surfing on-line, she headed out to Home Depot to purchase some rat poison. The internet gave specific instructions on dosages large enough to become lethal. Then she stopped at a uniform store to grab the final piece to the puzzle. Her mother was a diabetic, so she made a quick stop by her house and grabbed a needle and headed home to mix her concoction.

Tiara combined bleach and rat poison into the needle and was now in-route so Terry could meet his maker. Arriving at the county hospital during shift change, Tiara made her way to the floor, and was unnoticed since she purchased the same color scrubs the employees wore. After observing the nurse leave Terrys' room, she quickly decided to actuate her plan. Trying her best not to appear suspicious she made her way into his room. Terry appeared to be resting. With only on a limited amount of time, she walked over to his running I.V. and grabbed his I.V. port but was startled when Terry opened his eyes.

"Hey there," smiled Terry.

"Sir I'm here to give you the last dose of your antibiotic." Terry was assimilating her beautiful eyes. Although she wore a face shield he could tell through her eyes and her body that she was drop dead gorgeous. He noticed a rainbow tattoo on the back of her neck. As she grabbed his arm prepared to inject the lethal dose of poison, she heard footsteps which caused her to drop the needle.

"Hello there," a woman's voice greeted her. Tiara turned and quickly began walking out of the room, leaving the needle on the floor.

"Hey! You dropped the needle!" Terry shouted but she was gone. Tiara knew she had to get out of there fast or else she would be in jail. It didn't take long for the intruding nurse to realize that something was maliciously wrong about her visit and quickly ran out the room screaming for security. Unfortunately, Tiara was able to escape.

****

Not only was Donnie in mourning for Jennifer's death, he was pissed that the F.B.I. decided not to pursue an investigation considering the evidence against Passion wasn't incriminating enough. Yes, there were witnesses, police officers, judges and prosecutors murdered, but they had no concrete evidence that pointed towards Passion. Organizing a team of advocates would only be a fool's move. Without proper evidence, there would be a strong possibility she would win her case and file a huge lawsuit. Donnie knew in his heart she was behind the death of his sister and brother in law. He vowed to see justice served.

****

Passion left the office in a hurry. Someone tried to kill Terry at the hospital. No one knew who this person was and had no idea who was targeting him. He believed that whoever killed Mariah was trying to take him out as well. Mariah and Terry had killed so many people that they couldn't begin to pinpoint anyone who they may think could be behind this. Had it been someone who escaped their wrath and was out for revenge? They could only surmise possibilities. Terry was being guarded in the waiting room by a security officer when Passion arrived. She ran into his embrace and they held each other tightly for a moment.

"I don't know what's going on Pas but we gotta get out of here. The doctor said if I leave now I would be considered. A.M.A."

"Oh yeah that stands for against medical advice," said Passion.

"Well I don't have any insurance anyway, so I don't give a fuck. It's time to go baby. There isn't nothing wrong with me, but if I stay here I may die for real."

"Well babe let's roll," said Passion. As soon as the security officer stepped away for a restroom break, they quickly walked out of the room, scanning the surroundings until they were safely in the car.

"I've never saw this broad a day in my life. She looked like she was under thirty, but I couldn't really tell because she was wearing a face mask. You know the ones the doctors wear when they are about to do a surgery or some shit?"

"Damn she was on serious mission," said Passion.

"All I know is that I was able to see that she was an attractive lady, but I've never seen her before. Makes we wonder if she is the woman that Mariah was talking about when she called me on my voicemail shortly before she was killed. She said the chic was light skinned."

"Well Terry we now know we have to be skeptical of everyone we come in contact with. I mean we can't trust a fly boo."

Passion prepared a fulfilling meal for Terry while he was in the shower. They ate in silence as their thoughts ruminated. Terry broke the silence.

"Look, I refuse to wait another second for you to tell me what the hell is going on Passion." Dreading this conversation, she decided to lay it all out. She spoke about how Bill bugged her office, blackmailed her into sex and made plans to kill his own wife. Terry thought he was having a nightmare after hearing all of this. He pinched his arm.

"Why did you just pinch yourself?"

"I was hoping this was only a nightmare, but I guess not. So, let me get this straight, that cock sucker knew everything and was blackmailing you for sex and money?"

"Yes Terry, but guess what?" Terry listened. "He's dead now and before I go any further let me share with you a little more of my history. It's crazy how we've never touched base on our past. Seem like the last two days

224

we've both revealed some new information," said Passion.

"Yeah I agree."

"Well I' may as well tell you more and I'll try to make a long story short. I don't want to seem mysterious to you." Terry ears perked up as he was preparing to listen.

"Vice versa,' said Terry.

Two hours later Terry knew everything.

"So, this Tiara character.... Do you believe her story? Listen babe before you answer that, I just want you to understand the nature behind her actions and that's the only reason I'm probing. This is not one of those situations you should blow over baby. Trust is extremely hard to come by and agendas are far more common than we think they are. Tighten up Pas," said Terry with a serious look on his face.

"I totally understand honey, but we've burned the wire conversation. I stood there and watched her do it. There's no way she could have that recorded conversation without doing what she said she did. So, the answer is yes I trust my friend."

"Okay and what does she expect from you in return?"

"Nothing. We've been friends for so long but trust me, the sexual aspect of it all died a long time ago. She finally gathered the understanding that I don't go that route anymore. Our friendship is unconditional though honey."

"Umm hmm."

"What does that supposed to mean?"

"Nothing Pas, I got my eyes on her that's all. I mean she killed somebody for you, that's pretty deep if you ask me!"

"Well like I said before we've been friends since elementary school and she's a sweetheart. Now what I can say about her is that she respects our relationship. Just wait until you meet her before you judge her babe. Okay?"

"She seems a little dangerous and strange to me but, whatever. I'll leave it alone."

"Look who's talking! Mr. dangerous himself."

"Don't flip this on me woman. You still know how to flip flop a situation. Look at you, you tough!"

"Oh, shut up," laughed Passion.

"Ole flip artist Veland."

Passion looked Terry deep into his eyes and he stared back. "It sure does feel good to be here with you. Life is good with you baby. The thought of me having to live life without you killed me more than the damn accident."

"I love and missed you too Terry."

CHAPTER THIRTY-TWO

Passion invited Tiara over for dinner and gladly she accepted. Although Tiara was a tad bit worried that Terry would match her description to the woman at the hospital, she decided to take a chance. Since the face mask she wore covered most of her face she had strong doubts that Terry would recognize who she was. Nevertheless, she was prepared to take action. It was late in the evening when she arrived. Her hair was flat ironed today contrary to the Chinese bang ponytail she wore at the hospital. She was also sporting some Cartier frames with light blue metallic lipstick attempting to throw Terry off.

"You look beautiful girly, good to see you," said Passion. They hugged and walked down the hallway where Terry awaited. Passion introduced them, and Terry held out his hand. She reluctantly met his handshake with nervousness that he could sense.

"It's nice to finally meet you Tiara!"

"Likewise."

On the table sat a bottle of Ace of Spades.

"Pas got the Ace of Spades on deck. You've always kept a top of the line bottle of Champagne. Nothing has changed I see," said Tiara.

"Girl I don't change like the weather. I'm still the same ole Pas honey."

Terry poured everyone's cocktail and Passion broke the awkward silence.

"First of all, I'd like to present a toast. To friendship for years and years to come."

"Cheers," they all spoke in harmony.

"I trust the both of you with my life and I hope you guys realize that. There's absolutely no reason for you guys to feel threatened by one another. I love you both. Terry understands and respects our friendship Tiara and Terry, Tiara loves what loves me."

"Yes, I do," bluffed Tiara.

"Can I ask you a question Tiara?" said Terry.

"Yeah what's up?"

"Are you sure no one knows about our recorded conversation?"

"I'm one hundred and ten percent sure. I was convinced when that bastard took his last breath," smiled Tiara. Tiara was so gorgeous he had to break his stare. At that moment he understood why these two beautiful women were once in love with one another. What he could not understand was how this mesmerizing woman atrociously murdered two people in cold blood.

"Well what I'm worried about now Tee is who in the hell tried to kill Terry at the hospital. My guess is that whoever killed Mariah is the same person who tried to take Terry's life."

"Wait. Am I missing something? Who is Mariah?" questioned Tiara.

"Remember I told you about her Tee? She's the other assassin who suddenly and mysteriously popped up dead." said Passion. Tiara pretended to be bewildered.

"Oh my goodness. What about you Passy! I don't want anything to happen to you because of them." Her eyes left Passion and locked with Terry's. The unsympathetic reply was an innuendo of her hatred towards him.

"Nothing is going to happen," Passion suspired. "Let me go in here and check on the food."

"Do you need my help in there?" Tiara offered.

"Nah. While I'm in there, you guys can get better acquainted. I'll be right back."

Terry tried to ignite a conversation, but it was to no avail. Tiara remained insouciant and hardly responsive while gulping down the rest of her cocktail. As she reached down to pour another glass, her feathered flat iron flung forward. Terry's heart froze. He instantly noticed the same rainbow on the back of her neck as the culprits. His eyes began to assimilate her description again, but this time with skepticism.

He thought to himself. Same eyes, same figure. Then he pierced her eyes. "SON OF A BITCH." He screamed inside his head and looked away.

"Is there a problem?" Tiara asked.

"Why would there be a problem?" he nervously questioned?" She scrutinized him further without answering. He calmly got up and made his way to the kitchen. Grabbing Passion by the arm, he spun her around shushing her instantly.

"BABY IT'S HER," he frantically whispered. She's the bitch that tried to kill me." Before Passion could take his words in, Tiara emerged in the kitchen with a nine-millimeter pointed directly in Terry's direction.

"Okay Sherlock or should I say Inspector Gadget. I see you done figured it all out. Right now, I need the both of you to head back in the living room and have a seat. Hurry the fuck up cause I'm not playing." Tiara trailed them as they walked quickly.

"Please don't hurt us Tee."

"I'm not going to hurt you Pas......But this motherfucker right here is gone disappear for good. You are part of the reason my friend is going through this torture. It was the conversation she had with your bad luck ass that created this mess."

"Wait a minute Tee it's not his fault," Passion implored. Tiara hissed at Terry holding the gun with both hands.

"Passion you don't need him and just like a maggot, it seems like the drama has multiplied. You need to help me dispose of him and it will only be us. The way it's supposed to be." Tiara kept her focus on him.

"I love him Tee."

"I LOVE YOU! EVERYTHING I'VE DONE HAS BEEN FOR YOU. FOR US," yelled Tiara. She started breaking down. "Pas, don't you realize it can't be any other way?"

"I realize. I do," said Passion as she stood up from the couch.

"WAIT! Don't come any closer." Tiara warned her and aimed the gun at Passion. "I will shoot the shit out of you Passion if you go against me on this one." Passion froze.

"Tee, please put the gun down." Passion took a step closer." "I love you Tee. Listen to me baby please. Nobody in this house is going to get hurt. Okay?" Tiara began to reconsider.

"Okay," she whimpered and slowly lowered the gun. Then suddenly she felt like her and Passion had come to the end of the road and knew she was on Terry's side. Tiara figured that Passion would never leave Terry and their friendship could never be repaired. Her desire to kill Terry shifted in that moment. She now wanted to kill Passion. In a sudden moment she raised the gun and fired. Passion twisted and dropped to the floor.

"NOOOOOOOOOO!" Terry rushed her as another shot was fired. This shot whizzed pass Terry's face by inches. A quick struggle ensued before the gun was knocked loose. Tiara tried to run for the door and Terry ran behind her grabbing her by the hair and throwing her across the room. Tiara was a fighter and she forcefully kicked him in his balls causing him to lean forward. Then she made another attempt to leave the house, but Passion blocked the door.

"Passion get the fuck out the way you ole disloyal bitch!" Terry gathered enough strength to stand up and slowly crept to the door. Tiara turned around and Terry punched her square in the nose causing Tiara to bump her head against the wall and slide to the floor.

"That's why I killed your friend. You should've saw the bitch Mariah's face when I pulled my pistol on her fried ass. That was one ugly bitch right there." Tiara let out a loud snigger."

Terry began choking her. Tiara tried to pry his hands off of her but was unsuccessful. Tiara began to fade. Terry faintly heard Passion's voice.

"Don't kill her Terry!!!" Her demand made him snap back into reality but for Tiara's sake...she was five seconds too late. Her eyes were rolled in the back of her head when he had finally let go. Passion began to cry as she crawled over to her lifeless friend. Terry backed away and gave her a moment. A moment to mourn, cry and accept the fact that her childhood friend Tiara was now dead......

Tiara managed to shoot Passion in the shoulder that night, and Terry was arrested and held for seventy-two hours before being released. No charges were brought forth and the situation was written off as a self-defense case. Mariah was given a proper burial. The family was thankful yet curious as to why her ex-lawyer would display such generosity, not to mention attend her funeral. The Mariah Thomas and Tiara Wright cases wcrc now both officially......closed.

EIGHTEEN MONTHS LATER

Time had slowly passed since that disastrous night of Tiara's death. Passion and Terry had a small wedding ceremony at the courthouse and shortly after that, they decided to relocate to San Francisco California.

Several job opportunities were waiting as well as a chance to make a new start. Although Evelyn stayed with her mother back in Omaha, she traveled back and forth while Terry was in the final stages of receiving full custody of her.

They were blessed with a healthy six pound five-ounce baby boy that they both cherished more than life itself. Terry Junior had dimples and was the light that shined in Passion's eyes. No longer did being the best attorney in the world matter, little Terry was her thrill. Passion would cry when he became ill, even if it was a simple cold. Simply put, she was a nurturer at heart and was very overprotective. Refusing to hire babysitters, Terry stayed home during the day and worked at night. Their shared responsibilities seemed to work out perfectly. They enjoyed their newly formed family and took their marriage vows very seriously. Although Passion was currently handling a case in Colorado, Terry was back at home with the baby but missing his woman. All in all, life was good and it appeared as though life couldn't get any better.

CHAPTER THIRTY-THREE

Shantae had become a professional Stalker since the death of her husband. One detail she never revealed to anyone was that they were working on rekindling their marriage. He left her close to three hundred thousand dollars that no one knew about. Although he lived with Malaysia, Shakeem always took care of home and promised her that as soon as the last shipment was complete, he was going to break the news to Malaysia. He wanted his wife back. So Shantae's hopes were always high and wanted so much to live as a family again.

Her sights remained on Passion. Vivid memories of the way Passion smirked at her when the judge found Shawn not guilty pierced her soul. She hated her with every bone in her body for defending Shawn and setting him free. Although she took matters into her own hands and killed him herself, she equated Passion's duty to defend Shawn with spitting on her husband's grave. Shantae was dedicated to making her pay for what she had done.

Shortly after Passion relocated to San Francisco, Shantae decided to move to Oakland which is approximately thirty minutes away. As weeks went by, she studied their movements daily. There were plenty of opportunities to kill Passion, but she figured dying would be too easy. The vital information gathered by Shawn about how she made it to the top, would soon bring her skeletons out of the closet. She watched

Passion board her plane last week, and noticed the maid had a key.

Every Monday, Wednesday and Saturday around noon, Terry would stroll his son to the neighborhood Ymca and the maid would go feed the ducks down the street. Shantae felt it was now time to meet the maid.

It was a warm breezy day and ducks were scattered and moving in closer to the people that fed them. Shantae occupied a bench by herself, admiring the bird lovers. Glancing down at her watch the time read eleven fifty-six. She knew the maid would be arriving any minute. She lit her cigarette, took a few puffs, and flicked it away. At approximately twelve thirteen the maid arrived. Shantae zeroed in on her. She fed the ducks as if it was her responsibility.

"She must really have a good heart to do something like this on a daily basis." She thought to herself, however seeing her do this is what gave her reason to believe this plan may fail. She was prepared to find out. She accosted the maid and chatted freely with her about the birds and exchanged names.

Shantae discovered her name was Dorothy. Forty-six-year old single woman whose face was worn with stress lines. She knew that twenty-five thousand dollars would do her a lot of justice.

"Are you from here?" asked Dorothy.

"No, I haven't lived here very long but it's starting to grow on me. How about you, how long have you lived here?"

"You're a newcomer! Wow! Well to answer your question, I've lived here my entire life. Lucky me. I've always wanted live in Minnesota. I heard they have more opportunities there, but it is what it is." said Dorothy. The conversation paused while the birds ate from Dorothy's hands.

"What if I told you that our acquaintance here today was not accidental?" said Shantae. Dorothy was bemused. "I approached you today for a reason."

"Excuse me, no disrespect Shantae, but I don't like the sound of this conversation. It was nice talking to you, but I have to get back to work." Dorothy began to walk.

"How does twenty-five thousand dollar's sounds? I'm willing to hand over this cash to you right now for something in exchange." Dorothy stopped abruptly.

"What is this! Some type of childish prank?"

"Look at this ma'am. I don't play games at all." Shantae opened her briefcase and revealed the stacks of hundred-dollar bills.

"Oh my Lord what's going on here?"

"Look here miss, it's very simple. You can have this entire briefcase if you'll handover something I need."

"Well what might that be?"

"The key to their house." Dorothy couldn't believe her ears but could definitely tell Shantae was dead serious.

"Why do you want this key so bad? What are your intentions?"

"Nothing dramatic. I'm a family member and there's a few things in that house that belong to me. Rather than take her to court and lose since she's a famous lawyer, I'd rather get it back myself. When it's all over no one will ever know I was there. It would probably take years before she figures anything out."

"You know honey, I've spent my entire life remaining free from the law and to me, this all sounds like trouble."

"Look I know your concerned about someone getting hurt but that's not the case. My intentions are good, and I'd never do anything to jeopardize my own freedom."

"Something about this is telling me that if I accept this money, I will not be working there much longer. Can you promise me nothing crazy will happen?"

"Do I look crazy Dorothy? I promise!"

"You mind if I take a picture of you, for my protection?"

"How about I give you my phone number and show you my license. I hate pictures ma'am."

"Okay, that's fine." Shantae showed her driver's license, typed her phone number in her call list, and took the bait." It's hard for someone to refuse twenty-five thousand dollars in cash flashed in their face. The transaction was immediately finalized.

Dorothy went back to work twenty minutes later and finished her shift as usual. Her shift ended at seven pm. Through the bay windows, Shantae observed Terry placing his son in the bed while he browsed the internet for a couple hours. Shantae decided it was time to go home for the day.

Terry was dosing in and out while watching a movie when Passion called questioning his whereabouts for the day. Passion was homesick and began to cry.

"What's wrong boo? Don't cry."

"I'm sorry Terry I just miss you guys so much."

"Well the case will be over by the end of this week, right?"

"Yes, I know. I just want to hold him, and I want you to hold me"

"Well babe just hold tight. Junior and I will be right here waiting for you when you come home and I'm going to hold you all day and forever. You hear me baby. Man up Pas!" They both chuckled.

"I miss you silly."

"I get it babe I do. I know you're super lonely but don't forget you're the chosen one. With those big bucks comes a huge responsibility."

"You're right. I love you and give my Stookie butt a kiss for me okay."

"I already did."

CHAPTER THIRTY-FOUR

Terry was startled by his cell phone that he kept close by to catch Passion's call. It was eight eighteen a.m. He couldn't believe Junior allowed him to sleep that long without waking him up in the middle of the night. Passion greeted him with a smile through the phone.

"Good Morning handsome!!"

"Hey beautiful," smiled Terry as he struggled to open his eyes.

"How did Junior sleep last night?"

"Actually, his little butt slept all night. Usually he wakes me up to give him a bottle but maybe he's ready to start sleeping the whole night. I've been trying to put him on a schedule."

"Well look at my Mr. Mom. Where did you learn about baby schedules? Seems like you've been doing your homework."

"From my college professor."

"Okay I'm lost, can you catch me up to speed please. What college professor?"

"Google!" Passion and Terry both laughed out loud.

"You are so silly dude. Well I'm about to go to court, but you know I had to check on my two babies first."

Terry propped himself up in the bed and wiped the sleep away from his eyes. As he quickly glanced at the baby's crib, he did a double take. He froze for a second and Passions words weren't registering. His heart started racing and a dizzy spell washed over him.

"Oh my God!" yelled Terry.

"What? What's wrong?" He didn't respond. As he began to run from room to room, he dropped his phone on the floor. "TERRY!" shouted Passion trying to figure out what was going on. Terry grabbed the phone.

"Junior is missing!"

"What do you mean Junior's missing?" she asked frantically. Terry started panicking.

"Somebody has kidnapped our son. I've searched the whole house and where else could he possibly be? Passion. PASSION!"

Passion hung up the phone and immediately ran to the airport to book the next flight, unfortunately no flights were leaving for 3 hours. Passion explained to the flight attendant why this was an emergency as she broke down at the airport. The flight attendant observed the tears in her eyes and offered her a seat in a secluded private area until her plane arrived. Passion anxiety had reached an all-time high. At that moment she popped a Xanax to calm her nerves. Her tears along with anxiety caused her to drift off to sleep.

"Passion......PASSION!"

"Granny is that you?"

"Yes baby it's me."

"Oh granny I thought you were gone forever. I miss you so much."

"Well I'm resting my child, but don't you worry about me. Passion I know you been doing wrong and these angels in heaven are crying out right now. I've always been and will be your guardian angel. See baby when you do wrong in this world there's always a consequence. We may like to think that karma doesn't exist, but karma is all about sowing seeds honey. When you plant bad seeds, what do you think will grow? Baby listen, I want you to live in peace. Repent and ask God for forgiveness. I didn't raise you like this and no matter what happens from here on out, I want you to understand that no matter how your situation turns out to be on earth, it's never too late to turn your life over to the lord. He's the only one who can fix it baby. I gotta go now. I love you!"

"GRANNY GRANNY! GRANNYYY!"

"Ms. Veland. Ms. Veland. Are you okay? Your flight is ready," said the flight attendant. Passion jumped up and was startled as she woke up from the harsh reality that her conversation with her grandmother was a dream. She grabbed her purse and black shades and was anxiously ready to board her flight.

Terry sat on the couch waiting on Passion as the San Francisco Police department filled his house searching for evidence. Reporters were loitering outside taking advantage of a breaking news story. The F.B.I. had finally arrived and began to prowl and set up shop as if they were renting out the place.

Considering this family was rich, they expected a ransom was in the making. One agent asked where the maid was and since there was no forced entry they considered her to be a suspect. Shortly thereafter the maid arrived and was taken into custody for questioning. An interrogation ensued but she didn't tell them anything that was useful to the investigation, but her skittish behavior was alarming, and they decided to hold her for the forty-eight hours they were afforded. Passion arrived a little before three pm full of hysteria. Terry consoled her as much as he could but the thought of junior being hurt had them both in a lachrymose and weak state of mind.

CHAPTER THIRTY-FIVE

Hours had passed, and the only lead was the maid, but her story never wavered. Terry and Passion believed she was involved. Dorothy was the only person in San Francisco they had ties with, however assumptions were useless. The F.B.I. had their phone tapped and was ready to trace any calls that came through. At exactly seven twenty-two the phone rang. They ordered Passion to answer the phone. She wiped her face cleared her throat and then answered.

"Hello."

"Is this who I think this is?" asked the caller.

"Who are you?" Passion quivered.

"I'm the person with your child." The F.B.I. went into a slight frenzy.

"Listen, I don't know who you are, but whatever you want, I will give it to you. All I want is my baby back unharmed." Passion began to lose control as she leaned her head into Terry's chest.

"Stay calm baby you're doing good." Terry whispered.

"How does it feel to not know whether your child is dead or alive?" The address was retrieved by the F.B.I. and was clear on the other side of town. Law enforcement began to scurry.

"Look Passion. I can hear plenty of action going on in the background and I'm sure the police are all around you. I also know that this call is being traced and they are on their way to me right now as we speak. Oh but guess what?"

"What?"

"I'm glad you asked. Basically, everything is going as planned." Those words frightened Passion to the core. The F.B.I. was listening closely and aware that something more ominous than a ransom was at hand. A wave of panic and suspense rushed through the room and Terry held his head down in fear.

"What exactly is your plan?"

"Well let's just say I want the whole world to know the truth." The room was so quiet you could hear a needle drop. "See Passion this is not about your money at all. It's damn sure not about this little fucker I took from your house. This is about loyalty. Remember you clarified your loyalty when I came in your office that day. REMEMBER?" Passion remained silent. "Tell me MISSES LOYAL LAWYER, how much do you love your son. If you love your son, then the truth will be revealed. If the truth is not revealed, this little boy will die."

Passion trembled with terror and realized her ugly past was about to show itself.

"BITCH IF SOMETHING HAPPENS TO MY SON YOU WON'T HAVE TO WORRY ABOUT JAIL, CAUSE I'M GONE BREAK YA DAMN NECK WITH MY BARE HANDS!" Terry yelled.

"You better tell that son of a bitch not to say another motherfucking word. Jail doesn't scare me. I've been mentally incarcerated for some years now. You should know all about that Misses Passion."

"Who are you?"

"Who am I? Who am I?" asked Shantae as she chuckled. "I'm the woman who came to your office and offered you a shit ton of money to not defend the guy who killed my husband. If you knew better, you would've did better. See all you had to do was take the money and neither one of us would be here today. By you representing that coward bastard, you spit on my husband's grave and tore deep into my soul by embarrassing me in that courtroom. Do you know who I am now?" Passion tried to find her voice as she muttered.

"Yes, yes I do. Shantae I was only doing my job. It was never personal." Terry and Passion made eye contact and knew that the past was about to swallow their future. Terry dropped his head in a hopeless gesture.

"At this point my dear, I don't care what happens to me. My destiny is to avenge my husbands' death and my wrath will destroy everyone that opposed his demise.

Shantae's house was surrounded and bull horns were blaring.

"If the cops attempt to stop my plans, your child will die first and then I will kill myself. IS THAT CLEAR?" Shantae yelled. "Your best bet is to tell them to back the fuck off right now." Passion delivered the message and it was conveyed to the surrounding agents.

"What's your plan Shantae?" asked Passion.

"I want you to confess your sins of murder. I know exactly how you made it to the top. Now It's time that everyone else hears the truth. I want the TV reporters in the room. No secrets. The absolute truth. So, if loyalty means everything, then you'll save yourself from listening to the sound of death from your very own child. I'll butcher this baby to death and that will suffice if you refuse to confess. Either way, I'll be satisfied. So, choose your loyalty." Passion began to weep while understanding what was happening. The karma that her grandmother spoke to her about in her dreams was showing itself at face value. At this moment she felt alienated from God and defeated by a life of sin. All of those morals and standards her grandmother spent so many years instilling in her had went away with the wind. Preparing to confess for the absolution of her soul, she took a deep breath and Terry held onto her while she sobbed.

"Baby we are tight like twix! Do you hear me baby? Passion look at me! We are tight like twix baby!" Terry softly grabbed her chin to make eye contact. "We will get through all of this together." Passion stood as the detectives had their tape recorders and cameras ready.

Without any tears left to cry she held onto Terry's strength ready to tell it all. While facing the officers and television reporters she cleared her throat.

"My name is Passion Lynn Veland and my confession here today is the absolute truth. I've always dreamed of becoming a famous lawyer. My grandmother raised me with morals, dignity, and respect. When I lost her several years ago, the values that were once embedded, had died as well. Addicted to the thrill of winning, I hired people to kill to protect my career. Judges, lawyers, officers, prosecutors, and witnesses are all dead because of my selfishness. Murder for hire is what I'm guilty of. The person I hired as an assassin is deceased. She was killed a while ago and her name is Mariah. She's never revealed who assisted her with these murders and thought it was best that I didn't know. I presented her with the victim's information, and she took it from there. My husband never knew of my involvement in such corruption and although you've kidnapped my child, I must say that I respect your dedication to your late husband, because I never knew what true love was until I met mine. All I ask is that you return my baby safely. Thank you."

Those were her final words before she dropped the phone and hugged Terry. She whispered in Terry's ears.

"No more tears baby. No more fears." They held one another firmly as law enforcement was preparing to arrest Passion at the scene. Shantae surrendered peacefully while Terry junior was retrieved unharmed. She was charged with breaking and entering, first degree kidnapping, and terroristic threats. Passion was arrested and charged with consecutive counts of contract murder for hire. For the sake of her son, she couldn't confess the whole truth. He needed at least one parent in his life. Terry was heartbroken but understood his wife's decision to save their sons' life as well as her soul.

Passion was sentenced to life without parole. She completely turned her life over to God and felt a sense of peace that she couldn't explain. Terry never left her side and kept hope alive that maybe one day a new trial could take place. Until then he brought little Terry to visit her twice a month and kept their communication strong with phone calls, pictures, and letters. Although she was once destined for success, her choice to live a sinful life had cost her everything but her life. Passion began advocating for inmates and was able to overturn some of their cases. No longer was she cold. She held on to her faith of knowing that she would someday see her grandmother again..........

THE END............................

BESTREADPRODUCTIONSLLC

Acknowledgments

Our kids Tiara Hardnett, Tiana Hardnett, Jamye Mitchell, Joseph Jones Jr, Mya Mitchell, and K. Henderson.

Our Sisters and Brothers. Ericka Veland, Jasmine Cooper, Tobias & Andrenika Teel, Valerie Thomas, Anthony Hardnett, Andre & Tamika Hall, Jerry Richardson, Howard Jr Hardnett, Juwan Thomas, Ken & Janet Thomas, and Cedric Williams.

BestRead would like to acknowledge

Phillip Hodges for that beautiful photo shoot. One of the best and very professional.

Marcita Carter for your assistance with proofreading. Admire your intelligence sista.

Pierre "**_Jiffy_**"**_Johnson_** for your Graphic design skills and professionalism!! One of the best. Thank you!

Jertaya Holley People tend to judge you from the outside, unaware of the bumpy road you've endured. You've overcome so many obstacles cousin and I'm so proud of you. When we decided to place someone on this cover, you were the first person that came to mind. Simply because of who you are inside. Your looks helped. Don't get that twisted. (Smile) I'm just amazed at how you agreed to help us and wasn't worried about what was next. (I knew you would help us for real). We gone be alright! Corey and I are extremely proud of the way you rocked this cover honey... We wouldn't have had it any other way!!! Love you and once again thank you!

Acknowledgments from Corey Thomas

First, I would like to give a shout out to Kevin. You inspired me to write my first novel by reaching out for my assistance with your novel. Even in such places goals, fruitful ideas, and dreams are born. To everyone who sat and listened to me narrate for hours. M.T., Dolla, Stacks, Knuckles, Peoples, Terry, K-Rocc, Rodi and all the ones I've missed, I genuinely appreciate all you guys. For your criticism, time, support, but most of all for your motivation.

To My Cousin Keepers
Ladon and D-Bear. You guys advised me on countless occasions to stay focused on my craft no matter what vicissitudes I'd endure. **Deandre Johnson** I done told you once before man, "Tea Tea is all mine man" LOL but seriously thank you for introducing me to my wife fam. Love is Love.

To my mother Theresa Thomas (Lady T):
You're a strong beautiful Queen and I love you more than words can express. There's no one on God's green earth that could ever take your place.

To my beautiful daughter Jamye:
I love you and I'm proud of the woman you're becoming. Keep up the good work.

To my mother in law and grandmother in law
Mama and Mama Myla, I'm so blessed to be a part of the family and thanks to the both of you for always being kind to me. I love you!
To my Uncle Dwayne Thomas: Thanks for sending me all those bible quotes and writing me when I was away. You

kept my spirit uplifted man and I will forever hold that close in my heart.

Acknowledgments from Tamiko Thomas

Gladys 'Veland' Morris (Mama) There are so many words that could describe you, but here's a few. Beautiful inside and out, Humble, funny, witty, spiritual, Non-judgmental, and I know I speak for all of us grandchildren when I say you are the best grandmother in the world. I Love you!!!!!

Myla Veland (Mom) God couldn't have placed me inside of the belly of a better woman. Even though I came out raising hell, you never turned your back on me. I've always admired your patience and loyalty. Thank you for always believing in me and supporting me. You're awesome and the best mother in the world. I Love you!!!!!

Eva Veland (Auntie) I still remember those college talks you would have with me when we rode in the car. Even though that was the last thing on my mind, those conversations still motivate me to this day. You've always supported positivity and I've always admired the woman in you!!!Love you!!

Lisa Veland (Auntie) Sometimes I think you've been waiting for me to get on some kind of way, (smile) But just knowing that you knew your niece was something special, made me believe so as well. Thank you for believing in me, I love you.

Trish Shepard (Teacher) God placed me in that classroom to show me how to believe in myself. I know I speak for all Flanagan's High School alumni by saying that we love you! You taught us to have higher expectations.

Angela Banks (First Lady of Pleasant Green) I called you in tears at six in the morning waking you up out of your sleep, in all kinds of distress. That was a moment I truly felt like giving up. You cried and prayed with me and at that point I realized you were a special kind. Seem like God was speaking through you. Thank you for being there as that strong woman in my time of need. I love you.

Samiya
My first grandbaby. My beautiful princess. I love you boo. You're going to do great things. I'm claiming it!!!

Tiara, Tiana, and Joseph
My beautiful children! I love you guys so much and I'm so blessed that God gave me you!!!

Mama T
I love you dearly mother in law and I love your son to death. Everything will be alright!

To Everyone!!!We love you and Thank you for your support in advance.

Please feel free to visit our Facebook and Instagram pages to like and follow us. **_Best Read productions LLC_**

TO MY WIFE!!!

I scream this shout out to my beautiful wife and best

friend Tamiko Thomas.

You're everything in a woman that I could ever want.

Smart, strong, sexy and although we've had our up and

down moments, through every trial, our love has prevailed.

Our future is perfected by God boo.

I admire your desire to keep our dream alive, and no

one has ever showed me the dedication that you have

and I cherish it.

This is the beginning of our goals being fulfilled, but

most of all a dream that you and I together, have seen through.

I love you honey bunch.

Team Thomas 2018

BestReadProductionsLLC for Life

To My Husband!!!

There were so many Stumbling blocks, obstacles and pitfalls designed for our relationship to fail, but by the grace of God we made it through. They say a family that prays together stays together. We didn't realize that when we held hands and prayed together every night, we were building a solid foundation that no one could tear apart. NOT EVEN US!!!!!

We have experienced the good bad and ugly. BUT GOD..............

You're my best friend, my king, my leader, and my co-worker. (Smile) Intelligent, wise, handsome, and I thank you for allowing me to combine our dreams together to start this book company. Thank you for forcing me to look up words and the definitions. (Smile)

Thank you for having patience with my (STRONG BLACK WOMAN) syndrome.

God has a purpose and a vision for your life. He knew that at some point along the way, you would need a woman (Help meet) that could love you unconditionally as well as push your vision. (That would be me)!!!!! (Smile)

Our lives are intertwined through destiny and I thank God for you, for us, and for the ups and downs that allowed us to understand what true love really means. I love you!!!!!

Babe our teamwork made the dream work!!!!!!!

Team Thomas 2-12-2018

BestReadProductionsLLC for life

Words from Tea Thomas

This Novel is dedicated to my late grandmother

Mrs. Gladys Marie 'Veland' Morris.

(Aka) Mamma Our Matriarch and Queen. You passed away October 2, 2017 and left us all with amazing memories. You showed us how to love unconditionally and the true meaning of faith. A firm believer in God's word you never passed up a chance to help someone who needed you. You would give your last if that meant making someone else smile. You kept all of us grandkids together growing up. Our lives will never be the same without you. Thank you for showing us morals and values that we still use in our everyday lives today. Certain things such as: Treat people how you would like to be treated, prayer changes things, and giving is better than receiving. We can't compare to you mamma!! You are irreplaceable! We love you and miss you with our soul.

You are our Angel and we know you are smiling down on us every day! I know God said, "Well done good and faithful servant."

Rest in Heaven

www.ingramcontent.com/pod-product-compliance
Lightning Source LLC
Chambersburg PA
CBHW071136260626
47162CB00003B/808